OBJECTS IN MIRROR

RONDER THOMAS YOUNG

OBJECTS IN

MIRROR

ROARING BROOK PRESS

BROOKFIELD, CONNECTICUT

Published by Roaring Brook Press
A division of The Millbrook Press
2 Old New Milford Road, Brookfield, Connecticut 06804

Library of Congress Cataloging-in-Publication Data
Young, Ronder Thomas.
Objects in Mirror / Ronder Thomas Young.
p.   cm.
Summary: In a maze of school assignments and interpersonal relationships,
sixteen-year-old Grace tries to decide who she is.
[1. Identity—Fiction. 2. Family life—Fiction. 3. High schools—Fiction.
4. Schools—Fiction.]
I. Title.
PZ7.Y8767 Ge 2002
[Fic]—dc21   2001041712

ISBN 0-7613-1580-2 (trade edition)
1 3 5 7 9 10 8 6 4 2
0-7613-2600-6 (library binding)
1 3 5 7 9 10 8 6 4 2

Book design by Filomena Tuosto
Printed in the United States of America
First Edition

For Glenn,

for the past, for the possibilities, forever

OBJECTS IN MIRROR

1

Grace scanned the buses for familiar faces. Every day the drivers parked in a different place. Random spots couldn't possibly be easier than set ones. Clearly the plan was to keep everyone confused.

"Grace!" Allison's voice cut through the crowd. Grace whipped around. "Over here!" Allison's hand fluttered through the window of a little red car. Grace ran over and looked inside. Allison nodded toward the track. "Back gate's open." She patted the passenger seat. "Hurry, before everybody else figures it out."

Grace got in and stroked the leather seat. "Is this yours?"

"At the moment." Allison swerved to the left and zipped out the back gate. Grace didn't even know you could get on the main road that way. Usually the cars just lined up and idled in the parking lot for at least ten minutes. "Dennis says it's for me to use, but it's really just his excuse to have a sports car sitting in the driveway." She looked at Grace and laughed. Big black-lined eyes and smudged lips jumped out of her pale face. "Midlife thing."

Allison called her parents Sue and Dennis instead of Mom

and Dad because they were actually her aunt and uncle. Her real mother was Dennis's sister. "She ran off to Europe when I was a baby," Allison had explained. "So Sue and I," Allison emphasized, "aren't *actual* blood relations."

Grace unzipped the front pocket of her backpack and pulled out a folded piece of paper. "Saylers sent me another threat." She opened the note and read, "You must clear up your scheduling conflict with me personally, or I must continue to mark you absent every day." Grace shook her head. "Some girl delivered it to me in math class."

"What a nut case." The wind blew Allison's blond hair over her face like a veil.

"It's not as if I *changed* my schedule." Grace settled against the door and caught a glimpse of her own windblown hair in the side mirror. That's why girls in magazines always look so good, she thought. Wind machines. "I did exactly what they told me to do—"

"First mistake," Allison said.

"And they totally screwed up their own plan."

The wheels squealed around the curve. Grace straightened up and tugged on her seat belt. "It wasn't as if I was on her roll. I went up after class and told her she didn't call my name, so Saylers just *penciled* me in." She twisted a strand of hair around her finger. "Whose fault is that?"

Allison laughed. "It's always our fault." She leaned into a sharp turn. "Always."

Grace shook her head. "She doesn't know me. I don't know her. Why would she—"

"Teachers are the same as parents," Allison said. "It's their job to threaten you, to accuse you"—she flipped up her thumb—"to keep you under their thumb." She shrugged. "You hungry?"

"I need to get home."

"I'm paying."

Grace suddenly resented the red car. "I've got money," she snapped. "It's not that."

"Okay." Allison turned onto Campbellton Road. "So that's your dad's place?"

Grace looked up at the sign—MORRISON'S GARAGE AND BODY SHOP. "I guess so," she said.

Allison looked at her. "You guess so?"

Grace watched Jack pull a white Cadillac into the left bay. "Well, you know," she said, "my dad can't work anymore."

"But he owns it, right?"

Grace nodded.

"That's what counts." Allison pulled into Grace's driveway.

Grace could see her father peeking through the front window. She remembered how he used to leave the house every morning at seven. "I'd better get this day started," he'd say. "It's not going to happen without me." She looked over her shoulder at the garage. She had believed him, but since his stroke, it did. It happened without him.

"You know what?" Allison said. "My birthday's in three weeks. On the nineteenth. I'll be seventeen."

Grace nodded. "Oh, yeah?" She glanced at the house. The curtains in the front window moved. He was watching. She squeezed the door handle. "We ought to do something, me and you and Diana."

"Yeah." Allison leaned over and touched Grace's arm. "You can throw me a party."

3

"I don't think so." Grace laughed. "I'm not big on parties."

Allison held up her hands. "But I need you," she said, "to make it a *surprise* party." She pushed back her hair. "A surprise party's more fun."

"But," Grace said, "if it's your idea—"

Allison shook her head. "Not for me. For everybody else." She nodded. "Everybody gets so psyched. Totally different energy." She sighed. "So, obviously, what I need is for you to, you know, front the party."

Grace opened the door. "I am the wrong person." She swung her leg out. "Believe me."

Allison reached over and tugged on her vest. "Just think about it," she said. "And don't tell anyone."

"Okay." Grace pulled away and got out of the car. She wanted no part of it, but she was still impressed that Allison would just flat out make such an outrageous request.

"Especially not Diana."

Grace bent down. "How come?" *Especially not Diana?*

"Oh, you know. Diana's so committed to the real and the true."

Grace nodded and straightened up. "Thanks for the ride."

Allison leaned closer. "Which is great," she said. "I love that about Diana. It just wouldn't work in this situation." She straightened up and changed gears. "Okay?"

"Okay." Grace closed the door and watched Allison back out of the driveway. She'd had a birthday herself only a couple of weeks ago, and it had never even occurred to her to mention it to Allison. Grace and Diana had done just what they always did on their birthdays. Gone to a movie. Eaten a pizza before and ice cream after. The three of them had done a lot of things together since the summer, but Allison wasn't a part of their old routines.

Grace stumbled up the front steps and banged open the door. Her father rolled his chair away from the window and contorted his mouth into what Grace had come to believe was a smile.

"Who was that, Grace?" Her mother stood in the kitchen doorway. She didn't look at her daughter, but rather at the rubber ball she was squeezing in her right hand. Her arthritis was acting up again.

"That was Allison," Grace said. "You remember her. She came over back in the summer with Diana."

Her mother nodded. "Oh, yes." She looked up from her hand. "You missed the bus?"

Grace's two-year-old niece, Patty, ran down the hall into the front room, right smack into the wheelchair. As far as Grace could tell, her father didn't even flinch. "No," Grace said. "She just gave me a ride."

"That's quite a car," her mother said. "What is she? A senior?"

"No," Grace said. "She's a junior."

"This is the Allison in your history class?"

Grace nodded. How on earth, she thought, did her mother know that? Grace might have mentioned it, but Mrs. Morrison was usually too distracted to hear anything she said. These days it seemed the only time her mother looked directly at her was when she was angry.

"She's a junior in a sophomore class?"

Now Grace saw where her mother was going. "Allison's really smart. Last year she went to a private school up in North

Carolina, but . . ." Grace lowered her backpack to the floor. "Well, she has a hard time getting up in the morning, and history was first period, and so she slept late and missed too many classes."

Her mother's expression fixed flat and dead on Grace's face. Grace felt as if she were trying to explain something *she'd* done. "She's really smart, though. Even though she's repeating history, they put her in an honors class." Grace cleared her throat. "She lives in the big yellow house across from—"

"Right," Mrs. Morrison said. "The rich girl." She turned to Patty and beckoned with her finger. The little girl galloped over and pushed past her into the kitchen. Mrs. Morrison looked at Grace. "Her daddy's that big lawyer?"

Grace sighed. "Yeah." She looked over at her father. His eyes shifted away, back out the window. "Did you see how she backed right down the driveway, without any trouble?" Grace said. "Angela's just lazy. She doesn't have to cut through the grass the way she does."

Mrs. Morrison's mouth twisted. "Don't be smart," she said, and turned into the kitchen to coo at Patty.

If her mother would only pay attention, Grace thought, she would see that Grace *was* smart. Too smart to drop out of high school and run off to California, like her sister Sophie, and for sure too smart to get pregnant, like her other sister, Angela, without getting married. And, for that matter, too smart to sleep through history class, if she was ever lucky enough to be sent off to some private school.

Mr. Morrison redirected his head in a way that suggested he wanted Grace to come over. She put her hand on his stooped shoulder and leaned down.

With his left hand, her father slowly and awkwardly pulled a note out of his shirt pocket—he couldn't quite get his right one up that high.

Grace took it and read his new, loopy scrawl. "Water the grass." She straightened up, crumpled the paper, and nodded. "Okay, Dad." She ran out front and turned on the sprinkler. It was slinging too far to the left, over onto the Henshaws' side yard, so she turned it off, tugged it a bit to the right, and then tried again. Perfect. Grace looked up at the window. There he was. She nodded and smiled.

They hadn't gotten any rain in three weeks. Grace should have thought of watering the lawn herself. All those days he'd been at the window when she came home from school, Grace had imagined her father was watching for her, but he'd just been worrying over his grass. Same as before the stroke.

Same as her mother, who might seem to be looking at Grace, but all she ever really saw was Sophie and Angela and all the trouble that came before. Grace was going to be paying for their mistakes until the day she died. Or escaped. Whichever came first.

2

Grace read the note again. *"You must clear up your scheduling conflict with me personally, or I must continue to mark you absent every day."* Abigail, who was still in Saylers's class, told Grace that she'd explained to the teacher what had happened, just like Grace had asked her to, but that Saylers continued to call out her name every day. "And every time she says your name," Abigail said, "it looks like she gets madder and madder."

Kennedy rapped her tight little fist on the board. "Clear your desks," she said.

Grace saw her fingers crumple the paper into a ball. She looked up. She saw it whiz past Kennedy's head and bounce off the board. What Grace really did, though, was carefully fold and slide the paper into the front pocket of her backpack. School might not have taught her much else, but she had learned the importance of documentation.

Grace took the test from Kennedy and slumped lower in her chair. She skimmed the insulting little quiz. Each problem was followed by the question "How did you arrive at your answer?"

"Remember," Ms. Kennedy said. "I want to see complete sentences."

Grace zipped through the problems and then went back and jotted beside each one, "I worked it out in my brain." She twisted the hair off her neck and whistled up into her damp bangs.

"Man," Tyrone said. "It's hot in here." His long legs spread longer and wider in the aisle.

Ms. Kennedy tapped her lips with her index finger. "The temperature is perfectly fine, Tyrone," the teacher said. "Get to work."

Grace walked up the aisle and noticed that some of the kids hadn't done anything other than doodle in the margins of their paper. She laid her test on the teacher's desk.

Ms. Kennedy raised her eyebrows. "That was quick," she said.

"It's just review, right?" Grace asked.

Ms. Kennedy patted the pale puff of hair over her ears and sighed. "Yes," she said. "It's review."

Donnie Wayne's head jerked up. "Review!" he yelled. "Nobody ever taught me this stuff!" Usually Donnie sat in the desk behind Grace, but Ms. Kennedy always moved him to the front for quizzes.

The teacher waited for the wave of giggles to break before she said, "Then, Donnie, it isn't review for you."

Grace sat down and closed her eyes. School had a different answer for everybody, and not one of them was ever the whole truth. She opened her eyes and glanced at Tyrone's test. He hadn't made a mark on it, but he was making Kennedy wait for it all the same. On the surface, it looked as if Tyrone just didn't care, but from sitting beside him every day, Grace had come to appreciate how much solid effort he put into messing with Kennedy.

Grace looked at Saylers's note again. If she'd just slipped out of class that day and kept her mouth shut, Grace wouldn't have to be bothered with this stupid thing. But how was she supposed to know the woman was insane? She decided to settle this, once and for all, today. Even if it made her late for history, Stubblefield would let it slide. She put the note back and fumbled around for her copy of the Japanese alphabet. She settled on the symbol *JI* and drew three careful copies of it before the period ended.

At the tone, Tyrone winked at Grace and eased his way up to the teacher's desk. Ms. Kennedy's eyes ran down his blank paper. Her shoulders dropped. She raised her eyes, frowned, and shook her head. She didn't say anything, though.

Grace shoved out into the hall with the rest of the class. Saylers didn't have a regular classroom—she pushed around one of those portable desks like Kennedy—but most of the English classes seemed to be in the C Building.

Even though the back door was always locked, Grace figured Ms. Kaye would open it for her. She tapped on the glass. Ms. Kaye's classroom was dark. Probably met in the Media Center today. Ms. Saylers rounded the corner and looked dead at Grace. Grace smiled, waved, and tapped again. Saylers stared. She moved her hand in a slow circle and pointed to the left. Grace stared back at her.

"Go around." Saylers didn't bother to say the words out loud; she merely mouthed them and turned away.

Grace sucked in a deep breath. All Saylers had to do was press down on the lever to open the door. Grace could tell her, *personally*, that she'd been given the wrong schedule. That it was all a mistake. And that would be that. Grace grappled with her backpack and pulled out the note. Saylers probably didn't recognize her. She slapped the paper against the glass. Too late. Saylers turned and disappeared around the corner.

Grace gave the metal door a couple of sharp kicks before hustling over to the annex. She opened the locker, and Allison's stash crashed to the floor. One basic rule, Grace thought: big things on the bottom, small things on top. Grace had shelled out eighteen dollars of her own money for one of those locker organizers to make it easier, but she knew she couldn't complain too much. The schedule screwup had put Grace in the wrong homeroom for the first two days, and by the time it was straightened out, all the lockers had been assigned. This locker had been assigned to Allison, and Grace was lucky that Allison had offered to share. She crammed the jumble back inside, raced down the hallway, and slid into the desk behind Allison, right after the final bell.

Allison nodded at the front of the room. Stubblefield wasn't even there yet. "I don't have the car today." She arched her eyebrows. "Dennis needed it."

Grace shrugged. "Okay." It wasn't as if she expected to ride home in some red sports car every day. Wasn't as if she even wanted to.

"I've got drama club anyway," Allison said.

Grace nodded.

Stubblefield rushed in and dropped his case on the desk. He raked his hair back, but it fell right down again. "Okay, people," he said. "What have you got for me?" The kids pulled out their papers. Mr. Stubblefield sauntered up and down the aisles collecting them.

Stubblefield's long fingers pinched the corner of Grace's

paper and pulled it out of her hand. She looked up. Stubblefield nodded and smiled. Allison extended her arm and presented her paper. Bangles clattered to her elbow. Stubblefield chuckled.

When he was done, Stubblefield snapped open his case and dropped the stack of papers inside. He settled down behind his desk. "Okay, people," he said. "Open up to page 157." He looked tired. Probably worn out from traveling to Phoenix over the weekend to be the best man at that wedding. That was the single biggest difference between regular college prep and honors classes: You knew way more about the personal lives of the teachers in honors classes.

Stubblefield kept Grace's attention for a while, but Allison gradually pulled her away. Allison stretched out into enough space for three normal people, and her white-blond bob brushed the edge of Grace's desk. Grace watched Allison's knee nudge poor little Charlie Adams's butt. He glanced over his shoulder at Allison. She winked. He smiled and squirmed back around. Allison hunched down and did it again. Charlie didn't turn around. Allison extended her fingers very close to the back of Charlie's spiky hair and examined her black lacquered nails. Charlie shook his head.

Grace smiled. At first she'd wondered why Allison was always messing with him, but Charlie seemed to like it. Probably the only attention he'd get all year.

"No." Stubblefield held up his hand. "I'll have them on Friday. I promise."

Grace sighed. That was the only problem with Stubblefield—he was always late getting their papers back to them. Last week that cluster of girls up front had been speculating that their papers were late because he was having problems at home, that maybe his wife was giving him some sort of trouble.

"How'd they come up with that?" Grace had asked Allison.

Allison had tapped a shiny blue nail against her temple. "Wishful thinking." She had nodded at Grace. "He is awfully cute, don't you think?"

Grace had squinted at those silly girls. "Yeah." She shook her head. "But he wouldn't—"

"Sure he would." Allison gurgled out her low laugh. "If you set it up just right." That last bit she said loud enough for everyone, including Stubblefield, to hear.

Set it up just right. Grace looked at Stubblefield perched on his desk. All of the other kids slid out of the scene. Allison was up there touching his arm, moving closer. Grace saw herself. Standing. Perched. Moving in. The images flashed rapid-fire, like when the slide carousel went berserk in biology. Grace shook her head and squeezed her eyes shut.

Stubblefield tapped his pen on his desk. "You see the connection, right?"

Grace straightened up. She nodded along with the others and tried to pick up on the regular world again.

Allison folded her arms together and curled into a suddenly smaller person. She could do that in an instant. Cut from large to small. Happy to sad. Stubblefield's voice diminished in the distance. Grace settled back and watched Allison like a movie.

3

Patty arched her back and pushed out her belly. The buckle popped out of its lock. The car seat straps flew open. Angela slammed the back car door. "I don't have time for this." She climbed into the front seat and clenched the steering wheel with her fists.

Grace pushed up on her knees and reached back to tap the little girl on the nose. She locked the buckle and slid back down into the seat. "You can't just let her bounce around loose back there."

"I know. I just didn't want you to miss out on one of your superior moments." Angela plowed through the grass. "Where to?"

"Diana's." Grace looked back at the lawn. Angela had really torn up a spot. Of course, even that would probably end up being Grace's fault. She could hear it now.

Her mother would sigh and say, "Well, why was the ground so wet?"

Grace would explain, "Dad asked me to put on the sprinkler."

Her mother would look away and shake her head. "Well,

you knew Angela was coming." Angela had a sweet deal. Everyone knew she was going to screw up, so it was up to everyone to keep it from happening. And if you didn't, considering Angela was Angela, it was your fault. A very sweet deal.

Angela leaned into the rearview mirror and smoothed her lip gloss with a finger. "Well, I can't pick you up," she said.

Grace squinted at the mirror outside her window. "I've got a ride home." She rubbed her chin. She couldn't see anything, but it felt sore. If she didn't give it some attention tonight, there would probably be a pimple there tomorrow.

"As long as Mom knows, because I do not want to hear about it later."

"Mom knows." Along the bottom of the mirror were printed the words, *Objects in mirror are closer than they appear*. She looked over her shoulder at the car behind them. It was true.

Angela bobbed her head in time with the song on the radio. She rounded her lips around an "Oh yeah." Her gum dropped into her lap. She groped for it. The car drifted into the left lane.

"Watch out!" Grace yelled.

Angela swerved back, deposited the gum into the ashtray, and giggled.

"Let me drive," Grace said. "It would be safer."

"You?" Angela snorted. "You don't even have a license."

Grace rested her head on the seat and closed her eyes. Before the stroke, her dad had promised to take her to get her license on her sixteenth birthday. Now all deals were off. Her mother was always too nervous or distracted or rushed to let Grace get behind the wheel, much less take her for the test.

Grace opened her eyes. Her sister pulled a strand of

bleached hair out from her French twist and smoothed it around her chin. She checked herself in the mirror, wrinkled her nose, and tucked it behind her ear. From now on, Grace thought, when people asked her if she had any brothers or sisters, she should just give them a flat no. It was closer to the truth than yes. Sophie had run off when Grace was just a baby. And as for Angela, Grace had begun to ignore her altogether. It was easier than trying to understand her.

"Bird!" Patty screeched from the back seat.

Grace hunched down and followed Patty's finger. It was a big one, soaring behind the hospital.

"Yeah." Grace nodded. "Bird." Patty spent so much time at their house, she seemed more like a sister. Grace could say she had one little sister named Patty, and it would be as good as true.

Except that Grace's mother was too old to be Patty's mother. In fact, she was really too old to be Grace's mother. Even back in fourth grade, when Grace's mom brought cookies to the class, Diana thought she was Grace's grandmother.

"No," Grace told her. "That's my mother."

"She can't be," Diana said. "She's too old." Back then Mrs. Morrison hadn't been impossibly old, but Grace could see why Diana had thought that. Diana's mother, Kate, still braided her hair and shot hoops in the driveway.

"I know," Grace said. "But she's my mother just the same."

Angela stopped in front of Diana's house. Patty squealed and clapped her hands. Grace turned around and grabbed her fingers. "Bye, Patty." She opened the car door. "Thanks, Angela," she said.

Angela nodded. "You're on your own now," she said.

Grace sighed. "I know."

Kate opened the door. "Hello, Grace." She pointed down the hallway. "She's back in her room." She shook her head. "You might not recognize it."

Grace passed what the Henrys called the big room. Diana's brother's leg and arm were slung over the back of the couch. The television blared. "Diana!" Ted yelled. "Those cookies are mine!"

She stopped. "It's Grace." She stepped back and held up her hands. "I'm clean."

Ted's feet slapped onto the floor. His head shot up. "Grace." He shook back his hair. "I haven't seen you at school," he said. "Which lunch do you have anyway?"

"Second."

He nodded. "Oh." He aimed the remote and switched to a music video.

Grace waited a moment, but apparently he was done with her. She continued down to the last door on the left and looked inside. Diana sat on a round red rug, with her legs spread almost in a straight line and her arms stretched above her head.

The rug was new. Or at least new for Diana's room. The edges were frayed and faded to pink. The wraparound desk and four-poster bed were gone. A squat twin bed stood in one corner. A smaller, plainer desk and chair in the other. Instead of gauzy yellow curtains, the window was covered with skinny white blinds.

Diana smiled. "Isn't it so"—she lowered her arms—"Thoreau?"

Kate was walking down the hallway with a basket of

laundry. She halted at the door and said, "Isn't it just so ragtag ugly?"

"Mom," Diana said, "we don't go in for all your frilly stuff."

Kate shrugged and walked away. Grace looked at the window. The blinds were dingy and bent at the ends. She thought Diana might have taken them out of the back room in the basement. She sure hoped those beautiful yellow curtains weren't stuck down in that breezeless room. The best thing about them was their flutter.

"Their generation was supposed to be so liberated, but they're still stuck in that girly girl thing."

Grace shrugged. "You've only got one chair, though."

"So?" Diana folded her legs into a lotus position.

"Thoreau had three, right?" Grace said. "One for himself, two for company."

"Oh." Diana shook her head. "One for a friend, and one for company." She waved that idea away. "My friends sit anywhere. The floor. The bed."

Grace plopped onto the little bed. "Where'd you get this?"

"It's the bottom half of Ted's old bunk bed." Diana leaned over, pulled a long plastic container from under the bed, and opened it. It was stuffed with loose photographs. She pulled two off the top and held them up, one on each side of her face. "Check out these do's." She waggled the photo on her left. It was Diana's school picture from the fourth grade, with that dopey ponytail sticking up out of the top of her head. "My mother was a cruel and unusual woman back then," she said.

Grace pointed at her own photo on the right. It was all nose. "So," she said. "Look at me." She shuddered. "I was as good as bald." That was the year her mother had simplified her own life by cutting off Grace's hair.

"Hey." Diana dropped her photo and gathered her hair on top of her head. "Bald is way cooler than this." Tight auburn curls splayed out of her fist like a bouquet. "So anyway," she said, "Ted had to make a delivery over there yesterday." Ted made deliveries for an office supply warehouse.

"Where?"

"Calhoun Elementary." Diana extended her right leg. "And that collage of all of us is still up in the front lobby."

"You're kidding," Grace said. "After all this time?"

"Yep." Diana thrust the picture of Grace as a bald, bony fourth grader at her. "This is your legacy," she said. "Esteemed member of the Calhoun Street Elementary Charter Class."

That's where they'd met, in the fourth grade at the brand new Calhoun Street Elementary School. Grace had been dumped from Redan, and Diana had been shoved over from Henderson.

At the first recess Grace and Diana had both leaned against the chain-link fence and watched the other kids scuttle over the new plastic playground. "At Redan we didn't have a fence," Grace said. "We had woods."

"You miss your old school?" Diana had asked.

Grace shook her head. "No," she said. "And I won't ever miss this one either."

Diana had thought that was a wicked funny thing to say. She sat down in the dirt and with a stick drew a picture of the playground monitor. Grace squatted beside her and laughed. Ever since that moment they'd been "best friends" even though Diana didn't like those words.

"Girls who talk about best friends," Diana said, "are all about who isn't. Not who is." Which Grace knew was brilliantly true, but that was still the phrase she used in her own head.

At the end of that first year at Calhoun, the principal had put on a little ceremony and slapped their goofy pictures on the wall. When they were twelve, the district lines were redrawn again, and they had to change middle schools, but no one made too much of that. And then last year, just when they were over the shock of high school and settling in, their school was downsized, which sent Grace and Diana to the mega high school on Highway 81. The newspaper had referred to them as *overflow*. "Overflow," Grace had said. "Like from a toilet."

"Your math class any better?" Diana asked.

Grace slid her clogs onto the floor and pulled her legs up on the bed. "It's like," she said, "every day after lunch I have to march through the gates of hell." She shrugged. "I don't know what I did to deserve that class."

"You're overflow," Diana said. "They stuck Wendy Simpson in there at first, too."

Grace blinked. "Wendy Simpson? The newspaper girl?" Wendy Simpson had been editor, or at least in charge of something, on the newspaper in their old school.

Diana nodded. "Yeah." She touched the side of her nose. "With the stud."

"You know her?"

"I saw her at the coffee shop and was asking her about school and stuff, and she said her mother had to come in and pitch a fit with the principal to get her into Frankel's class."

"Frankel?"

Diana began shuffling through another stack of photographs. "She said he's real good." She held up one of the photos. "You ought to get in there."

"How am I supposed to do that?" Grace leaned over and snatched the photo. Seventh grade. At least she'd gained control of her own hair by then. "I don't have anybody to pitch a fit for me."

That's how Allison had said she got into honors classes despite her bad grades at Winston. Dennis had demanded it. "He told the principal he didn't care what their policy was," she had said.

Diana had giggled about Grace's overflow line at first, but she'd used it to beg Kate to let her try homeschooling this year instead of going to the new high school. "I'm tired of being sludge for the system," she said.

"That really hit a nerve," Kate told everyone.

Grace had tried it on her own mother. "Well, that's just disgusting," Mrs. Morrison had said.

At least her words worked for somebody.

4

Grace blinked at the green glow of the clock. Four fifty-nine. She wiggled her head down into her pillow. Just before she closed her eyes to go back to sleep, though, the shadowy juniper on her dresser caught her attention. The bonsai, she thought. Stubblefield's assignment.

"There are only two stipulations," he had said. "That the object be from another culture, and"—he had paused and looked up at the ceiling as if he were searching for the second one—"and it must be something you find in your own home."

"I'd take those wooden shoes," Diana had said, "that my mom got in Amsterdam."

"Yeah," Grace had said, "but I've got to find something in my own home." She actually had to *do* the assignment. Grace noticed that Diana seemed to enjoy talking about assignments way more now that she didn't have any.

Grace had been stumped, but she could see that the bonsai would work. Even though it didn't technically come from anywhere else—the pot was from the discard shelf at the Art Center, and the juniper was a scrawny one her father had dug up from under the big tree—the idea of it was from Japan.

That might not fly with some teachers, but Stubblefield, Grace knew, would get it.

Grace rolled out of bed and turned on a lamp. She spread yesterday's newspaper on the floor, lowered the plant onto the paper, and sat down beside it with her scissors. She opened her legs, pressed her left foot against the closed door and hunched over the juniper. She'd been neglecting it since school had started.

Cutting carefully, right next to the stem, Grace opened up and curved the scraggly top and bottom. Then she scooted up on her knees and clipped the edges, following an imaginary curve from top to bottom, as if she were drawing an S. She folded her head down to the base and cleaned out some fringe. She rocked back onto her heels and laid the scissors on the floor. The first rays of sun cut through the window.

Grace stood up and lifted the plant back onto her dresser. She ran her finger around the crackled blue-and-silver rim of the bowl. If Cheryl the potter hadn't left this pot behind when she moved to Charlotte, Grace would never even have thought about making a bonsai. She would have just dragged all the uprooted junipers into the woods like her father had told her.

She traced the shiny white Japanese characters on the front of the pot. That's what led her to the Japanese dictionary in the library in the first place. As far as she could tell, they represented something about water. Grace sighed.

She had liked Cheryl the potter. Her hair was baby-fine blond, and her clay-splattered jeans must have been, like, a size zero, but she had this large, friendly laugh. And her fingers were so long. Grace had loved watching them slide around the wet clay on the wheel, turning slimy gray lumps into things like this pot. What a fabulous life Cheryl the potter must have, that she could discard what had become the most beautiful thing Grace owned.

Grace opened her bedroom door. A load of clothes spun in the washing machine down in the laundry room. Her mother was already up. Seemed like she was always up. Grace sprinted across the hall to shower. She was blowing her hair dry when the phone rang. Grace turned off the dryer and straightened up. Her dad's chair rattled down the hall. Ever since that break-in at the shop last month, he went white every time the phone rang. A call this early was liable to give him another stroke. Her mother rapped on the door. Grace peeked out.

"It's for you." Her mother gave her a hard look to let her know she was thinking the same thing—that a phone call so early in the morning could kill her father, and, of course, since the call was for Grace, it would be her fault. "Someone from school."

Grace reached out and took the phone from her. "I'm not dressed," she whispered. She closed the door and sat down on the toilet. "Hello."

"Grace?" Allison. "I'm not going to be at school today. Would you go by Greene's room and pick up the chemistry study sheets for me?"

"Are you sick?"

"No. I'm just not going," she said. "You don't have to talk to Greene. The sheets are in that box outside her door."

"Okay."

"I really, really appreciate it," Allison said. "I don't know why she can't just test what's in the book." Allison lowered her voice to a whisper. "Hold on." She came back at a normal level. "Sue must have forgotten something," she said. "She thinks Dennis gave me a ride to school already." She laughed. "And who knows what Dennis thinks."

"You need anything else? Any homework?"

"No. I'll come by for the sheets."

"I work this afternoon."

"I'll call." Allison hung up. Grace laid the phone on the toilet seat and finished with her hair. When she opened up the bathroom door, her mother was waiting in the hallway.

"What were you doing up so early?" she asked. "Didn't you finish your homework last night?"

Grace rolled her eyes. "Yes." She shrugged. "I just woke up and couldn't go back to sleep." There had been no point in trying to be so careful and quiet. Her mother was always listening. Patty let out a whoop from the kitchen. "Is Angela still here?" Grace asked. She was thinking that maybe her sister could drop her off at school on her way to work, which would give Grace time to deal with that Saylers thing before first period.

Mrs. Morrison shook her head. "Angela came by so late last night, we just let Patty sleep over." Her mother said it as if it were a new thing, as if it didn't happen two or three times a week. Angela might as well move all of Patty's stuff over here and be done with it.

Grace went into her room and got dressed. She had time for a bowl of cereal before the bus came.

Standing at the bus stop, she considered how efficient it would be to get up at five every day. She felt like she'd already been through one day and was starting on another one. Two days in one. Once she sank down onto the taped and bumpy seat, though, the life drained right out of her. She wished she lived in a big house like Allison's, where somebody didn't smack into you at every turn, so you could do what you wanted and be who you were. She wished Diana was rumbling down Cameron Drive in her bus right now, same as Grace, same as always. She wished it was five o'clock. If she had it to do over again, she'd curl up and go back to sleep.

5

Grace had to walk down to the main road and catch the city bus to her job at the Art Center. It was just as crowded as the school bus, but its passengers were a different mix of people, of different ages, with different faces from the people she'd had to look at all day. Not by much, maybe, but the city bus was better. Better still, though, was the quiet in the Art Center before the afternoon kids clamored in. Before Hannah, the director, knew she was there.

Grace nudged her backpack under the desk with her foot and plopped down onto the chair. She played the six messages on the answering machine and wrote them down. Three were for instructors; she put those in their proper boxes. Two requested class schedules; she added the addresses to the mailing list. The last one was from Diana.

"Grace, it's me," she said. "I won't be by this afternoon. I was there all morning. Did you see my pot? Check the shelf. I've got to do some math today, or my mom's going to kill me."

Grace went back to the studio. There were three pieces in Diana's cubicle, but she knew which one Diana meant. The wet one with the zigzag rim. Grace touched one of the points very lightly. She'd never seen one done exactly like that before.

In the hall Grace met Hannah, who held out a stack of blue papers. Grace took them. She could see her afternoon was set. Fold and label the winter class schedules for mailing.

Hannah's salt-and-pepper hair slipped out of the knot on top of her head and frizzed around her thin face. "So Diana said she couldn't come by this afternoon," Hannah said. "She was on the wheel all morning." The first of the Primary Art kids clamored through the door. "It's so quiet here in the mornings."

Grace settled behind her desk and slid the top schedule off the stack, folded, labeled, and stapled it. She yawned.

Hannah hovered beside her. "Late night?" she asked.

Grace shook her head. "Early morning."

Hannah smiled. "Diana was waiting when I got here today. This homeschooling thing is certainly wonderful for her art." She nodded down the hall. "Did you see the piece she did today?"

Grace nodded. "Yeah." She yawned again. "I like"—she moved her finger up and down in the air—"the way she cut out the rim."

Hannah nodded. More hair slid out. "That's what it is!" She pointed at Grace. "She has time for that kind of detail. She owns her time now."

"Must be nice," Grace said.

Hannah straightened the shoulders of her tunic. Grace admired Hannah's quirky, colorful clothes, but they always seemed just a little too big for her. "I think you'd enjoy this independent study idea yourself."

Grace flipped her hair behind her shoulders. "Well, of

course I'd enjoy it." Hannah examined the details of Grace's life the way Diana picked over Chinese food—slowly, studying the green stuff, and getting all excited over tiny things, like finding one little baby corn. She thought by now Hannah would at least know the obvious things about her. "It was my idea in the first place." Diana might be the one doing it now, but she had to be talked into the idea. At first Diana was afraid she might be too lonely if she didn't go to school every day.

"Was it?" Hannah shifted her hip against the desk. She slid one of the schedules off the stack and folded it.

Grace nodded. "Last year, in Health, we had to bring in a current event—"

"A current event?" Hannah asked. "For Health?"

Grace shook her head. She'd never been able to make sense of Health herself, so she sure wasn't going to try to explain it to anyone else. "Anyway, I found this little piece about homeschoolers lobbying down at the state capital for something or other." Almost everyone else, including Diana, had brought in the front-page story about the water main breaking downtown.

Hannah laughed. "Oh, I'm sure your teacher must have loved that."

"It was just Coach Lassiter," Grace said. "He didn't even read it. He just checked me off, same as he did the cheer-leader with the recipe."

"A recipe?"

Grace nodded. "Well, it was cut out of the newspaper, so . . ." It had surprised Grace, too, that the coach hadn't even commented on the subversive subject of her article. She had been, after all, introducing the idea of not going to school into his classroom. The afternoon before, when she'd found the tiny article buried back in section C of the paper, Grace had literally yelped. She had fantasized, as she carefully cut around the margins, that there might be some students gutsy enough to stand up and walk right out, once they realized they didn't have to be there. She had even imagined, as she slid the article into her binder, that it might be her. But none of the kids woke up enough to take it in. And Coach Lassiter had just checked her off and moved on to the next kid.

"Well," Hannah said, "some folks you just can't rattle."

Grace slapped a label on the next schedule. "Oh, no," she said. "Coach Lassiter was always going off about something. In fact, that very day he went on and on about how merely ripping your current event out of the newspaper, rather than neatly cutting it"—she scissored a square in the air with her fingers—"like me and the cheerleader"—she shuddered—"indicated a lack of effort, which indicated lack of character, blah, blah, blah."

"Well," Hannah said.

Grace threw one spent label sheet into the wastebasket and began peeling the second one. "Coach Lassiter," she said, "was an idiot." She waved the thought of him away with her hand. "But before that, Diana and I had never even heard of homeschooling."

Hannah nodded. "But then you decided not to—"

Grace's dark eyes narrowed into slits. "I didn't decide anything. Diana talked to her mother about it, and she thought it sounded, potentially, like a very creative and intelligent idea. I told my mother the same thing, and what she heard"—Grace tapped her ears with her hands—"was that I wanted to drop out of school and party and do drugs and give birth to illegitimate babies."

Some parents began to show up to wait for their children. Hannah straightened up and smiled at them. "Well . . ." She reached out her hand to touch Grace's, but one of the mothers pulled Hannah away.

Hannah was nice, Grace thought, but she did wish Hannah would stop analyzing and worrying over her. Last year, when Diana had first started taking pottery classes, Grace had been the one hanging around. She would sit on the floor in the front hall and read, and maybe play Ping-Pong out back with some of the kids waiting for their rides. When Diana got out of class, they'd go over to the bookstore or the coffee shop for a while before they caught the bus home. The situation was fine just the way it was, without Hannah's interference.

The smiling and saying hello to each other was normal. It was part of Hannah's job, as director of the center, to be friendly. But then there was that time Hannah had seen Grace outside the center for the first time, at the bookstore, and they had both paused in recognition and said hello.

That moment had pulled them beyond cordial. Grace would say hello first sometimes. Hannah would walk right over to her corner to make small talk and ask personal questions. Eventually, though, the attention began to annoy Grace.

"Do you think," Grace had asked Diana, "that she thinks I'll steal something if I'm left alone out there?"

Diana shook her head. "No," she said. "Hannah's like that with everybody. She's in therapy."

"So?"

Diana giggled. "Cheryl said"—Cheryl the potter had been

Diana's first instructor—"that therapy doesn't seem to be helping Hannah personally, but it's giving her a lot of ideas about how to help everyone else."

Hannah's idea for helping Grace was to offer her a part-time job sitting at the front desk, answering phones, registering students, and general stuff like that.

Grace scanned the class listing. For weeks before offering her the job, Hannah had tried to get her to sign up for something. Grace thought that might have been Hannah's plan—to pay Grace money so she could sign up for classes and give the money right back to her. At the time, Grace would have been happy to go along with that plan. She folded the schedule and peeled off the last label on the last sheet. Not anymore. As soon as she got her first paycheck, she found it made her much happier to hold on to her money. So far she'd added four hundred and twenty-five dollars to her savings account. Her new plan was to take a year off between high school and college to travel around the world. She pressed the label into place. "Done," she said.

Hannah heard her. "If you're done," she called out from her office, "you can cut out early."

Grace picked up about twenty of the unfolded schedules and slid them into the display rack. She pulled her backpack from under the desk and checked her watch. Twenty minutes before the next bus. Plenty of time to stop by the café. She was dying for a cream soda.

The front door rattled open. Grace looked up and flashed her work smile. "Mom," she said. "I didn't . . . I was going to take the bus." Mrs. Morrison had driven over to pick her up a few times, but she always waited for her in the car.

Her mother wore the saggy green sweatsuit she only threw on to work around the house. And her hair stood up the way it always did when she first pulled off her cleaning babushka. She wrapped her fingers around Grace's arm. "Let's go."

Grace shook loose. "Mom . . . ?" She looked over her shoulder.

Hannah leaned over and looked out her door. She frowned.

Grace threw her a smile. "My mom," she said. "Come to pick me up."

Mrs. Morrison clamped her right hand on Grace's arm. Little Patty hung and twirled from her left one. Grace pushed against them both to move them out the door.

"See you on Monday," Hannah called out.

"Don't be so sure about that," Mrs. Morrison said.

Grace jerked her head around. Hannah was still watching. She'd heard.

6

For the fourth time, Grace asked, "Mom, what is wrong?" For the fourth time, her mother didn't answer. She didn't even look at Grace. She yanked open the car door, stuffed Patty into the backseat, and buckled her in. Grace shrugged and climbed into the front seat. She locked her eyes straight ahead and her mouth into a tight line. Patty whacked her on the head with Mr. Fuzzy, her stuffed rabbit, but Grace didn't flinch. Mrs. Morrison slammed the back door, opened the front one and adjusted herself behind the steering wheel.

Grace slumped lower and shifted her gaze out the window. The skinny Tai Chi people filed through the open door of the Art Center. Grace folded her arms and waited.

Mrs. Morrison stared through the windshield and gripped the steering wheel. She didn't turn the key. She didn't speak. Grace straightened up. Maybe *she* was having a stroke. She remembered what Angela had said about their dad—Angela had been the one who had found him lying on the floor of the shop when he had had the stroke. "He just stared at me," Angela had told her. "Like a big fish." Grace reached over and touched her mother's arm. "Mom?"

Mrs. Morrison looked at her. That little uncombed clump of hair on top of her head bobbled. She still held on to the steering wheel, but with her right hand, she waved around a piece of paper. Grace tried to follow it with her eyes. Her mother's features twisted into her mean face. "I truly thought you were on a different"—her mother's voice wavered—"a different path." Her mean face collapsed into crying. Her whole body caved in. She covered her face with her hands.

Grace's mouth dropped open. She instinctively braced for suspicion and accusation, but this was unfamiliar. Grace's shoulders sagged and, to her own amazement, she began sobbing herself.

The paper fluttered from her mother's hand onto the hump between their feet. Grace wiped her eyes. She saw the Eastside High School logo. It was a letter from school. She picked it up. *Dear Mr. & Mrs. Morrison*, it began. It wasn't a real letter. The *Dear* was just part of a photocopied form; the *Mr. & Mrs. Morrison* was typed in fresh. The whole thing was that way. The *Due to excessive absence in* was part of the copy, and *English 271* was typed. The *As reported by Instructor/Supervisor* part of the form was followed by the typed *Peggy Saylers*.

Grace sniffed hard and snapped out of it. "Mom," she said, "this isn't anything." She leaned over and unzipped the front pocket of her pack, pulled out her folded current schedule and dug around for the wrong one. She didn't throw anything away anymore. Always carried evidence. She found it and gently pulled on her mother's arm. "Look."

Her mother looked. "See that second one?" Grace waggled the schedules. Her mother took them. She held the papers side by side, seeing nothing, but, at least, Grace thought, looking. Grace tapped the new one. "See," she said. "See how it says *corrected*?" She moved her finger down. "See where it says *English 271*?" She slid her finger to the right. "And *Kaye*?"

Her mother nodded.

"Ms. Saylers isn't even my teacher," Grace said. "This is all a mistake." For good measure, she leaned down, unzipped the middle section of her backpack and pulled out her last English test. "See?" She pointed to her teacher's name in the top right corner. "Ms. Kaye's my English teacher."

Mrs. Morrison blinked. She held the two schedules, one in each hand, and looked from one to the other. She straightened up and nodded. "Then why," she asked, "were you crying and carrying on like that?"

"Because"—she blinked—"you were." She slid the papers back into her pack and zipped it.

Patty shrieked and pushed against her straps. Mrs. Morrison closed her eyes and released a long breath. Grace twisted around, reached for Mr. Fuzzy and danced him in front of Patty. It worked. She was still loud, but she was happy.

Grace settled back down in the front seat. Her mother opened her eyes. "I think you'd better drive." She got out of the car and walked around to the passenger side. She tried to smooth her ragged hair with her right hand and held the left one up to hide her face.

Grace slid over and adjusted the mirrors and the seat. Her mother got back in beside her and hunched down. That was the only reason her mother was letting her drive—now that she'd remembered she was a mess, she didn't want to have to look into traffic and risk seeing someone she knew.

But then Grace didn't care why she was allowed to drive. She just wanted to make the most of it. She hooked her right arm over the seat and watched closely as she backed slowly out of the parking spot. Patty's head lolled against her car seat. She stared like a zombie and pulled ferociously on her thumb with her mouth.

Grace turned and focused hard on the road. Her mother didn't speak. She reached over and turned off the radio. Grace expected her to say something, but she didn't. Oddly, the silence seemed to pull the three of them closer than talking would have. Sometimes, especially with her mother, Grace felt like talking got in the way.

As soon as Grace turned onto Campbellton Road, she knew something was wrong. There were no cars outside the shop. The garage door was down.

Her mother looked at her and spoke her first words on the trip home. "We sold it," she said.

Grace slowed down and squinted up at the sign. MORRISON'S GARAGE AND BODY SHOP.

"We didn't say much about it, because you never know if these deals will go through." Her mother cleared her throat. "Of course, I know you've heard us talking."

Grace braked to a complete stop. "Sold it?" She had heard someone say something about selling the shop. Maybe Angela. But Grace certainly hadn't taken it seriously. The shop was like a person. Like family. She never really thought of it as a thing that could be bought and sold.

Her mother reached out and almost touched her arm. "He made a real good deal," she said. "But still . . . well, he feels like he's given up the one last real part of himself."

A car came up behind them, and the driver blasted them with his horn. Grace accelerated and pulled into their driveway behind a burgundy convertible. The license plate said *California*. She looked at her mother.

Mrs. Morrison nodded. "And your sister's home."

Grace looked in the mirror and saw that Patty was asleep. "Sophie?"

"Sophie," Mrs. Morrison said.

Grace loaded Patty into her arms and walked slowly past Sophie's car. The rear fender had been bashed. "Wash me" was written in the grime on the door. Long blue-and-white feathers and a string of crystals hung from the rearview mirror. Grace's stomach fluttered. She hadn't seen her sister in seven years.

7

The three of them—Grace, Allison, and Diana—were supposed to go to a movie on Saturday afternoon, but they couldn't nail down the transportation. Allison wouldn't have a car after one o'clock. A ride to the theater was no problem, but no one could commit to picking them up. And the theater they wanted to go to wasn't even on a bus line.

They settled on meeting at Allison's house to hang out and watch videos. Sophie had said she would take Grace over after lunch, but around eleven, Allison called. "I'll pick you up," she said.

"That's all right," Grace said.

"No," Allison said. "I'm on the cell phone. I'm turning onto your street right now."

"Okay." Grace hung up and bolted into the bathroom. She was still brushing her teeth when the doorbell rang.

Grace heard Sophie chattering in the front room. She heard Allison laugh. She sighed. She'd rushed so she could meet her out front, but since Allison was already in the house, Grace figured she might as well take the time to change into her clean jeans.

"Grace!" Sophie shrieked.

Grace rolled her eyes. "I'm coming." She wiggled the jeans over her butt and zipped. She slid her sandals back on, then kicked them off. She probably wouldn't be back until tonight, and the last few evenings had turned downright cold. She pulled her clogs out from under the bed, slid those on instead, and stuffed a pair of socks into her purse.

Grace rushed out ready to go, but Allison was settled on the couch beside Sophie.

"Look at these, Mom." Sophie lifted Allison's right hand lightly up toward Mrs. Morrison, who'd come in from the kitchen.

Grace's mother wiped her hands on the cloth hanging from her apron, leaned down, and either looked over or through— Grace could never quite tell which—her little half glasses.

Grace looked over her mother's shoulder. Allison's nails were painted midnight blue. The ones on the second and fourth finger glittered with silver stars. A matching crescent moon was on her thumb.

Mrs. Morrison reached down and actually took Allison's hand. "Now where do you find someone to do your nails like that?"

"She does them herself," Sophie said. "Can you believe it?" She took Allison's other hand. "You should open up a shop. You would make a fortune."

Grace jumped in. "And she does something different, like what . . . ?" She looked at Allison. "Every week?"

Allison shrugged and looked down. "Or so."

"Well, now," Mrs. Morrison said. "That must take up a lot of your time."

Grace frowned at her mother. She must just not be able to help herself, Grace thought. She just had to spin anything and everything off into the negative.

Allison knew just where to go with it, though. She looked up and smiled. "Well," she said in a soft voice, "being at a new school and all, I have a lot of time."

Grace's mother reached down and touched Allison's shoulder. "Oh," she said, "you'll be just fine."

It was all Grace could do to keep from laughing. Poor, pitiful Allison, she thought, might be new at school, but she was already president of the drama club and had the starring role in the fall production. And just last week she'd been asked to do caricatures of the teachers for the yearbook. Grace hadn't even known she could draw, but obviously someone did. Grace snapped her fingers. "Let's go," she said.

Allison stood up. "It was really nice to meet you," she said to Sophie. "And to see you again, Mrs. Morrison."

"We're just going to hang out over at Allison's, to watch videos and"—Grace shrugged—"and stuff."

"Call if you're going to be late." Mrs. Morrison glanced out the window. "Take it easy in that little car."

Allison nodded. "It's my dad's," she said. "So I've got to be careful."

In the car, Grace leaned back, followed the blue trail of Allison's fingernails on the steering wheel, and replayed the scene in her living room. She was happy that her mother all of a sudden seemed to like Allison—if it was true, it would only make Grace's life easier—but the speed of the turnaround left her a little dizzy.

Allison turned right on the boulevard. "Are you going by Diana's?" Grace asked.

Allison shook her head. "Her brother's dropping her off around twelve anyway." She tapped the steering wheel. "This will give us some time to talk."

"Mmmm." Grace punched up the volume on the radio. Time to talk. She wondered if Allison was still stuck on that party idea.

Allison turned into her driveway and parked in the back. Through the window Grace saw Dennis sitting at the round table in the breakfast nook. When they banged through the kitchen door, his head tilted slightly away from his newspaper. "Hello, ladies." He folded his newspaper and laid it on the table. "You do remember," he said to Allison, "that I need the car today."

"It's all right," Allison said. "I'll use the Honda."

Dennis shook his head. "It's in the shop, honey. Until Monday." His face tightened up as if he'd been struck by some sudden pain. "We went all through this."

Allison bit her lip. "Well, maybe Sue . . ."

Grace looked away and tried not to laugh. Allison was clearly messing with him. She'd told Grace all this last night, about how the Honda was in the shop, about how Sue and Dennis had to work, everything.

Allison climbed up onto the barstool. "Well, we can just hang out here." She looked at Grace. "Want to watch videos or something?"

Grace looked down at her feet and nodded. "Sure."

"Well." Dennis held out his arms and shook his head at

Grace. "Sorry." He looked at his watch. "I've got to run." He pulled his jacket off the back of a chair, slid it on, opened his briefcase, shuffled through some of the papers, then snapped it shut. "So," he said. "I don't know how long your mother's going to be, but I've got to depose two"—he dropped the case down to his side and held up two fingers—"very difficult witnesses that I've been after for weeks."

Depose, Grace thought. What did that mean exactly? Dennis talked like somebody off of a television show.

He grabbed the doorknob. "But we will have dinner. All of us. Together."

Allison moved a penny around on the bar with her index finger. "When?" she said. "What if I get hungry?"

"We will." He gestured toward the refrigerator with his case. "But, of course, if you kids get hungry, go ahead"—he nodded at the cupboards—"eat something."

Allison waved him out the door. As soon as she heard the door to his car close, she dropped her head down, slapped the counter, and convulsed with laughter. "See what I mean," she said. "He kills me. Like I need permission or instructions or whatever to eat."

Grace couldn't help laughing with her. It was mean to jerk him around like that, she thought, but, still, Dennis did come off pretty stiff and stupid. Maybe he just thought he had to try harder, seeing as how he wasn't her real father.

"Are you hungry?" Allison slid off her stool.

Grace shook her head. "My mom cooked pancakes this morning."

"She cooks breakfast every day?"

"On weekends mostly." She leaned on the bar and studied the lace curtains that hung from the row of windows that curved around the nook.

Allison nodded. "I don't think anyone here has ever actually cooked breakfast. We just get up and go on our way." She picked up the kettle and shook it. "Want some tea?" She held it under the tap to add some water, then set it back on the stove.

"Yeah." Grace walked over and fingered the delicate, droopy lace. "I love these," she said. "I saw a picture of some lace curtains in the newspaper last Sunday, and I showed them to my mother and told her how we ought to get some for our kitchen."

"Hmmm." Allison leaned against the counter with her arms folded. She squinted and frowned at the curtains as if seeing them for the first time.

"She said they weren't practical. She said, 'What's the point of putting something over your windows that people can see right through?' "

"Well"—Allison waved her right hand at the windows—"we don't get a lot of traffic back there."

"The point is, lace is pretty."

"Yeah, but you do have those folks living on that side, who could, you know, see right into your kitchen."

"I figure if people are the problem, you get rid of the *people*, not the lace."

"Yeah," Allison said. "That's good." She nodded. "That's real good." She opened up the cabinet and pulled out two massive mugs. "Get rid of the people." Allison laughed and looked over her shoulder. "Black or green?"

Grace looked at the mugs. One was red with blue stripes. The other one was yellow swiped with red and green and orange flowers. Like a faraway island. Like Tahiti.

"The green's fruity." Allison studied the canister. "Kiwi, I think."

"Oh," Grace said. "Black." She laughed. "I thought you meant the mug."

"Well," Allison asked, "which mug?"

Grace shrugged. "I don't care."

Allison turned and looked at her. "Sure you do," she said. "Which one?"

"The flower one," Grace said.

They took their tea into the front room. Allison folded herself into the chair beside the piano. "So, about the party," she said.

Grace curled in the rocker and wrapped both hands around her mug. "I don't know—"

"No." Allison held up her hand. "Wait." She took a sip. "Listen." She took another sip. "Parties are very efficient. They can also be dangerous. Surprise parties are the most productive and carry the least risk."

Grace laughed. "As long as they're planned by the guest of honor."

"Exactly." Allison nodded. "And anyway, only an egomaniac would wait around for someone else to come up with the idea, don't you think?"

Grace laughed. That was one way of looking at it. "I thought you said they were fun."

"They are. The party starts the week before. People are comfortable before they even get there." Allison set down her mug. "I've got it all worked out. I just need you to set it up."

Grace took a sip. What Allison said made sense, except for one thing. "I'm not big on parties."

Allison leaned forward. "Why not?"

Grace opened her mouth. She knew why not, but this was usually where Diana jumped in and listed all the birthday parties from hell they had attended until, in the sixth grade, they said *no more*. Ever. Grace could hear the answer, but, oddly, she couldn't articulate it in her own words.

"Listen," Allison said.

Grace tilted her head. It sounded as if a car had stopped out front.

Allison stood up and flourished her hand. "This house needs a party."

Diana tapped on the little square of glass in the front door. Just before she pulled the door open, Allison turned to Grace and touched her index finger to her lips.

Grace looked at the deep window seat in the adjoining room. There was another one like it in Allison's bedroom. A window seat was up there on Grace's wish list, way ahead of lace.

8

llison struggled with the ice cream. It was the big barrel size, like they had in freezers at ice cream shops. She set the first bowl on the bar. "Caramel Fudge Macadamia," she said. "Killer."

Grace moved the bowl to the table in the nook. The sunlight through the lace left shadows of circles and diamonds on the table; she traced them with her finger. "I liked it a lot," she said. "I thought the characters were just perfect."

Allison set two more bowls on the table and slid in beside Grace. Diana sat down opposite the two of them. "I did, too," Diana said. "Up until that point. Why would Bob have taken Quaaludes like that, from someone he didn't really know, given his whole attitude about drugs—"

"That's the irony," Allison said.

Grace winced. Diana thought people threw the word irony around way too much.

"No." Diana shook her head. "You can't just . . . invent irony. It has to come from a true place."

"She didn't say they were Quaaludes, though," Grace said. "She said they would help his headache."

Diana shook her head. "Yeah, but before that he was even down on aspirin, and—"

Allison licked her spoon. "Well," she said, "it is just a movie." She fluttered her lashes at Grace and sighed.

Grace bit down on a chunk of ice cream, fudge, and nut all at one time. She looked at Diana. Actually, what happened to Bob made a certain kind of screwy sense to her. On the other hand, she and Diana had agreed for years that to say a movie was "just a movie" was never an explanation and never okay. She looked at Allison. "But then that's no excuse," she said.

Diana slid a big bite off her spoon. She shrugged. "Of course," she said, "he was drunk. That was established." She nodded. "And his head was really killing him."

Allison spooned the last big chunk of Caramel Fudge Macadamia into her mouth. She giggled. Fudge glopped in the corner of her mouth. Diana laughed. Allison jumped up and brought the barrel over and scooped out more ice cream for everyone. "Dennis only eats one scoop at a time—never two, never one and a half—then puts down his spoon and pushes away the bowl."

Diana turned her spoon around in her mouth and licked it. "Very sensible," she said.

"Very anal," Allison said. "Dennis is Mr. Precision. He's compulsively moderate. He proceeds prudently." She reached up and clicked on the television tucked on the shelf. "Sue says his dad was the same way."

Grace ran the facts through her head. If Dennis's sister was Allison's real mother, that would make Dennis's dad Allison's grandfather all the same. "Your grandfather?" she asked, just to be sure.

Allison nodded. "He was a lawyer, too." She pressed down the button and zipped through the channels without looking at the screen. "And later on, a judge."

Grace scraped the sides of her bowl. "Is he dead?"

Allison shook her head. "Just in hiding. He's put so many people away over the years, he's paranoid, I guess. He's afraid they'll get out and come looking for him." She shrugged. "Just doesn't see people anymore."

"Not anyone?"

"Dennis goes down from time to time, but not me."

"Why not you?" Grace asked.

Allison shrugged. "Maybe he's afraid one of the desperadoes could get to me. Could pay me enough to take care of him once and for all." She raised her eyebrows. "Maybe he's right." She giggled. "He sends me these letters ranting about 'giving attention to my character above all else.'"

"So he sends you letters?" Diana said.

Allison slapped her hands on the table. "Oh, man, that's not all he sends me." She jumped up. "I'll be right back." She ran up the back stairs behind the pantry.

Diana laughed. "Oh, well," she said. "What's Sophie like? Beautiful? Like her pictures?"

"Yeah." Grace touched her chin with her finger. "So far, it's okay." Sophie had been home only a handful of times over the years. The way Grace remembered them, her visits had always started out slow and easy, then came down hard at the end, leaving bad feelings for days and days after she left. "The thing is, I'm not sure she's just visiting. Yesterday this huge"—Grace held her arms out to the side as far as they would go—"UPS box arrived from California, and when I asked her what it was, Sophie said, 'My worldly possessions.'"

A loud thud resonated through the ceiling. Both girls looked up. "Maybe Allison's mother isn't really in Europe," Diana whispered. "Maybe she's crazy and locked away upstairs, like in *Jane Eyre*." She tapped her fingers on the table. "Be right back." She went into the bathroom on the other side of the stairway.

Grace jumped up and padded down the hallway, past the dining room, to the bathroom beside the living room. She passed what Allison called the green room. Whenever Sue was home, she seemed to spend a lot of time sitting lotus-style on the daybed, hunched over her laptop, or talking on the phone. Grace slipped through the door and pushed her feet against the green-and-orange oriental carpet. Its design was an extraordinarily intricate vinelike affair. In one spot in the middle, it was worn through almost to the hardwood floor underneath. There were no curtains on the windows, just green wooden shutters covering the lower halves. Grace stepped out and continued down the hallway to the bathroom.

She closed the door and studied the details. The two tones of blue on the walls came together with a narrow strip of flowered wallpaper in the center. The framed, yellowing newspaper photo of the dog with the caption she still didn't quite understand. The violets on the sill and the stained-glass flowers hanging in the window. Best of all, the big, plush towels—a beige one, a green one, and a pink one—that didn't match anything or each other. Grace's mother bought a lot of things for the house, but it was always stuff that came in *sets*.

As Grace padded back down the hallway to the kitchen, it occurred to her that beautiful things, by definition, could never, ever come in matched sets. Beautiful things were rare and solitary. And you gathered beautiful things around you in spite of their color or age or whether or not people could see through them.

Allison and Diana were back at the table in the kitchen. Allison pinched a little gray velvet pouch with her fingers. "Hold out your hands," she said. Grace and Diana held out their hands. Allison sprinkled some of the contents of the pouch into each of their palms. Grace and Diana looked at the jewels in their hands. They looked at Allison. "He sends me these," she said. "They're real. Sapphires, rubies, and emeralds." She pointed to two in Diana's hands. "Those are diamonds," she said. "I'm going to use those for my wedding ring, with"—she pointed to some pale blue stones in Grace's hand—"the sapphires." She looked up. "Do you think that would be too much?"

"No," Diana said. "That would be beautiful."

Grace stared at the stones in her hand and shook her head.

Allison laughed. "Of course, maybe actually marrying someone would be too much." She fluttered her fingers. "Maybe I'll get the ring made up and just pretend."

Later that night, after dinner, Grace lay on her bed in her own house. In the living room, the television blared, and her sisters shrieked. Things did not have to be forever the same, she thought. Sophie could come home. Bob's head could hurt so bad that he'd chase it away with a fatal dose of Quaaludes. Maybe even Grace Morrison could throw a party, despite any decisions made when she was eleven years old.

The phone rang. Angela blasted through Grace's door and tossed her the receiver. It was Allison. "So," she said, "do you want to do it?"

Angela let out another yell. Grace pulled the memory of Allison's house—the ice cream, the lace, the window seat, the desperadoes, and the jewels—over her head, like a blanket. Allison was right. That house deserved a party. And, Grace thought, I deserve that house. At least for one day. She saw herself sitting on the daybed in Sue's green room. Climbing all the way to the top of the attic stairs. Snuggled in the window seat up in Allison's bedroom, waiting for the party guests to arrive. "Yes." Grace sat up. "I do."

9

During the week, Grace usually just grabbed something for breakfast on her way out the door, but this morning the entire family was crowded around the dining table. Since it seemed expected, she pulled out a chair and sat down. She looked over at Angela, who was cutting up a sausage link for Patty. Sophie reached over Grace's plate and grabbed the grits. Grace tried to remember another time they had all been sitting around a table like this, but she couldn't.

"Grace?" Angela said. Grace looked up. They were all staring at her empty plate. "You want a ride to school? Make a move."

Grace spooned a pile of grits onto her plate and swirled them with butter and salt. She nibbled on a piece of dry toast.

Her mother took a piece of toast, buttered it, cut it, and laid half on her husband's plate. Mr. Morrison looked at Grace and took a deliberate bite.

Sophie slid her tongue between her lips and shifted her eyes from her mother to her father and back again. "So," she said, "Daddy sold the shop. What exactly does that mean? Are we ruined? Are we saved? Are we rich? Are we poor? What?"

"We're retired." Mrs. Morrison's hand slid lightly over her husband's. "We're fine."

Grace remembered how whenever her father had driven past a cemetery, he'd point and say, "That'll be my retirement home."

Sophie bounced in her seat. "That's what you always say." She rolled her eyes. "We're fine."

Mrs. Morrison nodded. "And we always are."

Angela scraped away from the table and stood up. "I've got to go." She leaned down and kissed Patty on the top of her head. She looked at Grace. "You coming?"

Grace nodded, gulped her last bit of juice and followed her out the back door. To her surprise, Angela backed down the driveway instead of whipping around on the grass. Grace looked back over her shoulder to see if maybe Sophie's convertible had been in her way. Angela screeched onto the road. "We?" she said. "Can you believe that?"

"What?"

"Are *we* rich?" She shook her head. "Hey, I love Sophie. I wish good things for her. But, my God, she comes waltzing in after all this time, talking about the money and *we* and *us*—"

"Yeah," Grace said. She glanced ahead at the shop. The garage doors were up and people were milling around. How could everything be completely different and yet look the same? "But, are we?"

Angela was checking herself out in the mirror on the visor. She never could decide about that one bit of hair. Down the side of the face or behind the ear? "What?" She pushed it behind the ear and flipped up the visor.

If it were Grace, she would just tuck that strand away with

all the rest and be done with it. Sometimes it was all she could do to keep from reaching over and ripping the hair right out of Angela's scalp. She cleared her throat. "Are we okay?"

"Hell, yeah," Angela said. "That place was a gold mine." She slowed to a stop at the intersection and turned to Grace. "But exactly how many cars have you been under, Grace?"

Grace turned away and looked out the window.

"Mama and Daddy are a long way from dead," Angela said. "Their money is their concern."

Grace slumped down in the seat. Maybe Sophie did have a lot of nerve. She was thirty years old. Maybe she didn't have any right to walk into their life and start talking about "our" situation. But how was Angela any better? Little Patty spent more time with her grandmother than she did with her mother, and it sure wasn't always because of work.

Angela blasted her horn at a car that turned in front of her. Grace sat up straight. The noise seemed to clear her head. "Hey, Angela," she said. "I'm sixteen years old. I live here. They're my parents. It is my concern."

Angela nodded. "Well, yeah," she said. "I didn't mean you so much." She drove past the main drive at the school and continued on to the south gate. "Here?" she asked.

Grace nodded and pointed to the delivery area behind C Building. "Up there," she said.

Angela maneuvered the car up behind the dumpster. "You sure?" Grace nodded.

"Ms. Kaye'll let me in." She jumped out. "Thanks, Angela."

"Yeah," Angela said. "Good luck."

Grace nodded. She wondered if her mother had told Angela about Grace's attendance problem. Back when Angela was in school, it had been a joke, the way every single little thing that went wrong was someone else's fault. She had teachers who didn't like her, didn't listen to her, didn't understand her, and, in a few interesting cases, were jealous of her. The way this year was going, Grace wondered if maybe she shouldn't have taken Angela seriously at least once in a while. Now she knew that sort of stuff could happen.

Ms. Kaye came to the door on the first knock. "Good morning, Grace." Ms. Kaye adjusted her glasses. "What's the good word?"

Grace smiled. Ms. Kaye was so corny, but she still liked her. "Tautology," Grace said.

Ms. Kaye's lips, which were tinted the same creamy pink as her glasses frames, jumped into a smile. "Excellent." She circled the air with her index finger. Ms. Kaye was vocabulary mad. She had her students keep a vocabulary notebook to which they were required to add five new words every week.

Diana sneered at that assignment. "All she cares about," Diana said, "is that you all don't embarrass her come SAT time."

Grace agreed that was probably why they were doing it, but Diana wasn't there. She didn't know Ms. Kaye. Ms. Kaye cared about more than that. And even if it were true, Grace found tracking down the new words a kick.

"Thanks," Grace said. "For getting the door." The light was on in Saylers's room. Grace tingled as she walked through the door. As silly as it was, this screwy business hung in the back of her brain all the time. Finally, she could put it behind her and get on with her life.

The teacher sat behind the desk writing in a notebook. She

looked up and smiled. "Can I help you?" The question sounded kind and sincere, but, unfortunately, the speaker wasn't Ms. Saylers.

Grace took a deep breath. "Oh," she said. "I thought Ms. Saylers was in here first period."

"She is," the lady said. "I'm Carolyn Boone, her substitute."

Grace deflated. "Oh." The moment Ms. Boone had looked up, Grace had imagined something more definite coming out of her mouth. Something like, *Ms. Saylers is gone. Gone forever.*

"Will you be in one of my classes today?" the teacher asked.

Grace shook her head. "That's just it."

Ms. Boone's face crinkled into a smile. "What?"

Grace sighed. She had a few minutes to kill. She sat down and poured out the whole situation.

Ms. Boone shook her head. She nodded. Raised her eyebrows. Then, when Grace took a breath, she responded with the perfect words. "That," she said, "is the stupidest thing I've ever heard." She shuffled through several roll books. "Here we go." She looked at Grace. "You said third period?"

Grace nodded.

Ms. Boone ran her fingers down the list. "Here you are." She looked up at Grace. "In pencil." She flipped her pencil over and erased Grace's name and the marks after it. "She'll forget all about you now." She waved her hand over the papers on the desk. "And if she doesn't, with all the other stuff she's got to deal with, she's a psychopath." She shrugged. "More likely, though, she's just a bit obsessive." She nodded. "Okay?"

Grace nodded. "Okay." She watched Ms. Boone rotate the pencil with her fingers. "Thank you," she said and backed out of the room.

10

With a pencil, one woman Grace didn't even know—Ms. Saylers—had scribbled down Grace's name and caused all kinds of trouble. Then another woman, who was probably here for only one day, flipped her pencil over and erased the problem. A person's life, Grace figured, couldn't get much more insignificant than that. The image of the pencil turning over and over, from the pointy end to the pink eraser, dissolved into the scrawl of Grace's name appearing and disappearing, and burned in her brain all morning. Grace wasn't big on writing poems the way Diana was, but the whole thing did suggest poetry. She tried to work it out in the margins of her notebooks.

By lunch, though, Grace had figured out that maybe it wasn't that big of a deal, what Ms. Boone had done. That old, screwed-up schedule could still be in the computer for all she knew. Although it was always some human beings who took your forms and told you they'd take care of it, it was always what was in the computers that they used against you in the end.

Grace skipped the cafeteria and went to the front office.

Abigail, the student helper, was out front instead of the secretary, Ms. Munch. So far, so good. Ms. Munch never did anything without a load of questions and a pass of some kind. Abigail didn't care. Grace asked her to pull up her schedule, and Abigail just did it. She turned the monitor so Grace could see. Ms. Kaye for English.

"Could there be another one under my name?" Grace asked. "That has me in Saylers's class?"

"Another one?" Abigail frowned. "Why? It's not right?"

"Yeah, but"—Grace rummaged in her backpack—"I got this." She pulled out the letter.

Abigail looked at it, shrugged, and gave it back. "Don't worry about it," Abigail said. "It's just a screwup."

"Yeah, but is this letter in the computer somewhere?" Grace asked. "Because I don't want my mother getting another one."

"No." Abigail looked at her watch. "The teachers just fill in the forms and send them out as a warning. Nothing's put on the record until the end of the semester." She shook her head. "They screw up all the time. It just goes away."

Grace nodded. "Thank you so much."

"Whatever." Abigail went back to reading her book.

Grace had thought she'd have time for a slice of pizza, but there was a line. She bought an ice cream sandwich instead. It just *goes away*, she thought. Not much poetry in that.

After fifth period, Allison was waiting for Grace at the locker. "I didn't see you at lunch."

"I had to go to the office."

"Something wrong?" Allison folded her arms and leaned into the locker.

Grace shook her head. "No." She nudged Allison aside and put away her math text. "I just had to check on some things."

Allison leaned in and whispered. "Well, anyway, I found out that Ted's making a delivery to Dennis's office on my birthday. He always comes in the afternoon."

Grace pulled out her history book and straightened up. "Ted?" she said.

"Shhh!" Allison touched her lips. "So what you do is, you ask him to bring me to the party," she whispered.

Grace blinked.

"To *surprise* me." Allison bobbled her head. "If I show up, right on time, on my own, it'll look kind of suspicious, don't you think?" She nodded. "There's got to be a scene." She pushed her hands back and forth. "Some tension."

"Ted?" Deliveries, she thought. She looked at Allison. To her dad's office. "Diana's brother, Ted?" Allison's literature text fell off the stack of books and slammed onto the floor. Grace knelt down to pick it up.

"Oh, oh." Allison touched Grace's shoulder. "There's Tara. I've got to talk to her." She took off down the hall. Her lab binder slipped out onto the floor.

"Great." Grace straightened up, arranged the books properly—big ones on the bottom, binders in the side slot—and headed on to class. Allison and Tara stood outside the door, flipping through a paperback, shaking their heads and arguing.

Allison slid into her seat in front of Grace right at the tone. She turned around. "We're supposed to do a scene together for drama." She closed her eyes and shook her head. "She's stuck on this really pedestrian bit."

Grace nodded. *Pedestrian*, she thought. She smiled. Good word for this week's list. Ms. Kaye especially enjoyed common words used in uncommon ways.

Stubblefield rushed in and slammed his case on the desk. "Hello, people."

"What did you mean exactly?" Grace whispered. "About Ted?"

Allison shook her head, tapped her index finger on her lips, and turned around.

Grace stretched out her legs, chuckled at Stubblefield's opening joke, and took down a few lines of notes before she drifted into the white-blond screen of Allison's hair. It must be natural; she'd never seen even a trace of dark roots pushing through. Grace projected Allison's party. She saw herself drop her arm to cue the "Surprise!" She saw Allison affect a dramatic but believable response. Only she couldn't put faces on the people crowded around them.

Stubblefield tapped three dots hard on the board. That was his way of saying "This will definitely be on the test!" Grace looked up and quickly copied the remainder of notes from the board onto her page. "Remember, oral reports on Friday," he said.

Grace sighed. Stubblefield always went alphabetically. Sean *Williams* knew he'd carry over to Monday. Allison's last name was *Anderson*, so she knew she'd be up first thing Friday. *Morrison*, however, could go either way. A couple of absences would work her in on Friday; one nervous rambler could push her over into next week.

Allison stretched her arms over her head. Her bangles slid down and clanked together at her elbows. She brought down her arms and yawned. Stubblefield stopped talking and looked at the clock.

Grace smiled. Stubblefield was a good sport, a good way to end the day. The tone sounded. Grace searched the board for the page numbers of tomorrow's reading assignment, jotted them down, and jumped up.

Allison clamped her arm. "Wait," she whispered.

Grace shook her head. "I've got to go," she said. "I've got to work today." She had to stop at the locker, then run across the street to catch the city bus downtown.

Allison held onto Grace's arm. "I'll take you."

"It's out of your way."

Allison stood up. "Out of my way?" Allison said. "You know where I'm going?"

Grace laughed. "If you're sure," she said. Allison cornered Tara to discuss that scene again, and Grace went on ahead to the locker. When Allison caught up with her, Grace asked, "So did you change her mind?"

"Yes."

"How?"

"I told her it was the faculty's favorite audition scene at Winston."

"You should have told her that to begin with." Winston was apparently well known for its theater department. All the drama kids had been very impressed that Allison had gone to high school there. Grace and Diana had never heard of it themselves, but they had been very impressed by the fact that Allison had gone away to high school and lived there on her own.

"I only just thought of it." Allison winced. "I mean, it's not true."

Grace settled back on the soft leather seat of Allison's little car and closed her eyes. She tried to see how the Ted thing would work. He didn't really know Allison. It didn't make sense. She opened her eyes. "So, before the party, you'll be at your dad's office?" That was good. She had to be somewhere.

Allison nodded. "I go in all the time to use his computer. The Internet's so much faster than at home. You don't have to dial up or anything."

"So maybe your dad could bring you."

"My dad?" Allison shook her head. "Are you insane?" She laughed. "Fortunately, he won't even be there."

Grace didn't have to be at work until 3:30, so they stopped at Zino's for milk shakes. They sat outside at the picnic table to drink them.

Allison unfolded the scene. "I'll be there. Ted will be there. It makes perfect sense."

Grace shook her head. She still couldn't see it.

"How I get there, at just the right time," Allison explained, "is most important. Otherwise, people will be onto us."

Grace bit her lip. "I don't think he'll—"

"Trust me." Allison pumped the straw in her cup. "Just ask him."

Grace shook her head. "I don't think so."

"I know so." Allison slurped the last of her milk shake. "You're always over there. Just ask him."

Grace checked her watch. "We'd better go." She stood up. "Honestly, Allison, I don't see it happening."

"I do," Allison said. "And if Ted brings me to the party, he might as well stay for the party." She stood up and jingled her bangles back down around her wrists. "And if Ted's at the party, why wouldn't Mark and David Gillespie—maybe even Bryan Dunne—be there, too?"

Following Allison's logic was, for Grace, the same as playing chess. When it was time for Grace to make her move, she was always completely baffled, but when it was time for other people to move, she saw their strategy with crystal clarity.

Ted had taught Grace and Diana how to play chess when they were eleven—or tried to teach them. He'd gone through the moves a few times before he stormed off, yelling something about how girls thought they could make up their own rules.

"Ted should be easy," Allison said, "because he's a real sweet guy. You can just tell." She turned onto Murray Avenue. "And Tara. Get her in on it."

"Tara?"

"She's plugged into that whole drama group," Allison said. "She's the one who chatted me up for president of the drama club." Allison laughed. "I just stood back and let it happen."

Grace sighed. Before she got around to Ted and Tara, she had to run this party thing by Diana. That would either make it real, or the whole thing would blow up into nothing. In all the years they'd known each other, Grace couldn't remember ever lying to Diana. There was a very real possibility that she wouldn't be able to do it now.

11

Hannah juggled two purple panels down the hall. She blew the frizz out of her eyes. "Thank goodness you're here," she said.

Grace squatted and slid her backpack under the desk. "It's Monday."

Hannah leaned the panels against the wall. "Nevertheless," she said. "I'm happy to see you."

Grace stood up. "Oh." She shook her head. With everything else that had happened, she'd forgotten all about her ugly exit on Friday. "That was nothing." Suddenly she recognized the panels and snapped her index finger at them. "The puppet stage." She'd forgotten the Fall into the Arts open house coming up on the weekend, too.

"That's right," Hannah said. "I thought we could get that out of the way this afternoon."

"Okay." Setting up for open houses, festivals, and exhibits was Grace's absolute favorite part of her job.

It took both of them two trips to struggle down the hall with the oversized front and back pieces of the theater. "I tried skipping the whole puppet thing last fall, but every kid that came through the door—" She sighed. "One thing I've learned about kids," she said. "They demand continuity."

Grace nodded. She remembered how all the kids had squealed and clamored around when she'd set it up at summer camp. "What about the little curtains?" Grace asked. "And the trim?"

"All that's in the cardboard box marked 'Puppets' on the"— Hannah closed her eyes and wiggled her finger—"on the . . . top shelf on the left." She opened her eyes. "You remember how to do this?"

Grace nodded.

"Because I'll be attached to the phone all afternoon."

Grace knelt down to check behind the side panels for the *A* and *B* that indicated which one went on the left, and which one went on the right. Hannah watched her. Grace looked up. "I can do it," she said. "Really."

"I know." Hannah strolled into her office, but then turned and came back out. "Your mother does know you're here?"

Grace stood up. "Really, Hannah, it was all just a big misunderstanding. No big deal."

Hannah shrugged. "Okay, then." She went back to her desk, squeezed the receiver between her chin and shoulder and grabbed a pen. As far as Grace could tell, Hannah wrote down every word that anyone ever said to her on the telephone.

The center was particularly quiet because Ms. Huang had canceled her afternoon painting class; the only students were the three or four pastel people sketching in the studio. Grace could hear all of Hannah's phone calls. She called the people who were delivering the tent to discuss the possibility of setting up on Friday evening instead of Saturday morning. She called the caterer to determine that they would serve coffee in full-size cups, not those sample sizes like that cheesy outfit had done last year. She called the Primary Art instructor to remind her to have her students' work in Hannah's office by Thursday so that it could be included in the exhibit. From watching Hannah, Grace had learned that what was important in pulling off big ideas was the attention you paid to the little details.

When she had the basic structure together, Graced tapped the joints of the puppet theater with the hammer to tighten them. The curtains and fringe were wrinkled, so she got the iron out of the closet and pressed them on her desk—remembering from last time to lay them wrong side up to protect the nap.

Diana struggled through the front door with a big box and set it on the floor. She pulled out the flamingo marionette, unwound the strings, and walked it around. "I love this guy," she said

"I like the penguin," Grace said.

Diana nodded. "You almost done?"

"Almost." Grace tugged on the fringe to see if it was secure. "I've just got to log the new registrations." She sat down at her desk and pulled out the class book.

Diana set the flamingo down, picked up her box again, and brought it over to the desk. "Hannah said for me to put one of my pots in the exhibit. I think either this one"—she pointed at a purplish one with what looked like a sunburst inside—"or this one"—she pointed at a smaller smoky black one striped with white crackle. "What do you think?"

Grace hesitated. The purple was more dramatic, but the

little one was simple and intricate at the same time. She couldn't help remembering how long Diana had spent on that glaze; it had taken her more than an hour just to lay out the pattern stripes with strips of narrow masking tape. "They're both good," Grace said, but she pointed at the black-and-white one.

Diana nodded and picked it up. She gave the purple one another look before sauntering into Hannah's office. "Grace said this one, too."

Hannah held up a finger, eased the receiver into its cradle, and, with her black pen, slashed another item off her list. Then she said, "Great. Don't put it on your shelf, but rather on the"—she closed her eyes—"on the third"—she opened them—"the third one from the bottom marked 'Exhibit.'"

Diana disappeared back into the kiln room with her little pot and came back hugging a big blue one. "Hannah said I could probably sell this one to some country–kitchen–type lady."

"Yeah." Grace sat down at the desk and opened up the class logbook. "My mom would love it."

"Well." Diana held out the bowl. "I'd give it to your mother."

Grace shook her head and laughed. "You need money. My mother doesn't need another bowl."

Diana looked at her watch. "Isn't it time for you to go?" She lifted two pots out of her cardboard box, set the big blue bowl in it, stuffed newspaper around it, and arranged the smaller pieces back on top. "It's six."

"I'm almost done."

"Go." Hannah stood in the doorway of her office. She

nodded at the puppet theater. "It looks great." She waved her hand. "Really." She closed her office door, which was something she didn't usually do.

Diana looked at Grace. Grace shook her head. "She's all right." She pulled out her backpack. "She gets like this before an event."

Since Diana had a stash of pottery to take home, Ted was picking her up, and since Grace was on the way, Diana said he wouldn't mind dropping her off. "He said that?" Grace asked. "That he wouldn't mind?" She had heard him whine to his mother more than once about "being used," just because he had his license, and Diana didn't.

Diana pushed through the entrance of the coffeehouse next door. "Why would he?" She set her box on a table by the window. "Watch these," she said, "and I'll order."

Grace pulled two dollars out of her pocket and gave them to Diana. "Cream soda," she said.

Diana came back with the soda. "He said he'll bring mine over in a minute."

"You got a cappuccino?" The machine was sputtering behind the counter.

Diana nodded. "You sure Hannah's okay?"

"She gets like this," Grace said. "She's a perfectionist. And it's like Hannah and I are the exact opposite when it comes to these things. I like setting up, being by myself. Hannah calls that 'grunt work.' She likes the event."

The guy leaned over to set Diana's cappuccino on the table. His ponytail hung over his shoulder and wavered dangerously close to the cinnamon-specked foam. Diana and Grace watched it closely. It didn't touch. "Thanks," Diana said. She watched him saunter back behind the counter. She leaned over and whispered, "Do you think he's cute?"

Grace looked. She liked his hair. His shoulders were wide. His arms were thin but strong looking. Sinewy. And she liked the way his leather watchband fastened with rawhide strips rather than a buckle. "I guess." She leaned forward. "But don't you think he always looks so . . . so sleepy."

Diana arched her eyebrows. "Maybe," she said, "I could wake him up." She stuck her finger in the froth and licked it. "So will you have to be there on Saturday?"

Grace shook her head. "Hannah's got loads of volunteers for Saturday. Being in the middle of all that is everyone's favorite part, not just Hannah's."

Diana grinned. "So you're the opposite of everybody, not just Hannah."

"Especially Hannah, though. She'll be chattering and happy once the people show up and—" Grace stopped. She saw Hannah's tired eyes and heard her persistent telephone voice. She felt as if she were selling Hannah short. "Of course," she said, "Hannah's job depends on all those people." She shrugged. "I just show up, do what I do, and go home."

Diana held the fat cup with both hands and took a sip. She licked the foam off her upper lip and nodded. "Yeah," she said, "but have you ever noticed how Hannah gets prettier, the more people gather around her?" She leaned back and took up the cup again. "Hannah does love a party."

Grace straightened up. She licked her lips. Diana herself had brought up the word *party*. It was a sign. "Let's have a party for Allison," she said.

Diana frowned. "For Allison?"

Grace nodded. "A surprise thing. For her birthday."

"A surprise party?" Diana wrinkled her nose. "Like in a sitcom?" She shook her head. "People don't do that in real life."

"Yeah, they do," Grace said. "Remember how Allison's always talking about the party, the one when she left Winston?" Grace nodded. "That was a surprise party."

"Oh, yeah." Diana rotated the cup on its saucer.

"I think she feels like . . . like she's an outsider. Her classes are all off track." Grace held her hands out and moved them up and down like a scale. "Is she a sophomore or is she a junior."

"She's a junior," Diana said. "You just count up the credits, and—"

"I know. I don't mean technically," Grace said. "I mean how she feels."

Diana leveled her eyes on Grace. "Feels?"

Grace tried to stick to her prepared script. "She's got that whole acting thing going, but she doesn't feel like she's altogether a part of it yet, and—"

Diana cocked her head. "She's president of the drama club."

"But still," Grace said, "she feels like an outsider."

"Oh," Diana said. "That whole lonely-at-the-top sort of thing?"

"You're not at school," Grace said. "You don't know how she is." She settled back in her chair. Diana couldn't counter that. She wasn't there. She didn't know.

"Do you think," Diana asked, "that everything Allison says is exactly . . . true?"

"True?"

"The hermit grandfather and all that?"

"I don't know." Grace laughed. "She's got the jewels to back it up."

"And how she changed the gazelle story."

Grace shrugged. "Poetic license," she said. "It made for a better story for her report."

"It's the same thing." Diana leaned forward. "What if there never was a surprise party at Winston?" She slapped the table. "Or, what if there was, but it wasn't for her? It was for somebody else?"

Grace looked down and sighed. She couldn't counter that. Didn't really want to try.

Ted clattered a chair around and straddled it. He tapped his finger beside Diana's cup. "Suck that down," he said. "I've got to go."

Diana lifted her cup, but stopped before it reached her lips. She looked past them both. "Of course," she said, "if that's true, it's really even more of a reason to throw her a surprise party now."

Ted flipped back the tab on the plastic top of his to-go cup and took a sip. He leaned close to Grace. "She doesn't even like coffee," he said in a mock whisper. "She just likes to say the word." He fluttered his eyelashes and rolled the word out in a high voice. "Cappuccino."

Grace smiled. She liked the way he'd let his hair go long, waving off in a wild wedge.

Diana drained her cup and flicked Ted's head. "Okay," she said.

He stood up and nodded at the box. "Need help?" he asked.

"No." Diana picked up the box and walked outside.

Grace noted how, even with the bickering and complaining, Ted offered to help with the box. Maybe, she thought, Allison was right about Ted. Maybe he would be willing to help out.

Diana slouched silently against the passenger door for the first few minutes of the drive. Then she turned to Grace in the backseat. "Maybe you're right," Diana said. "It's a sweet idea."

Ted pulled up to the red light. "Well," he said. "What do you expect?" He turned around and looked at Grace. "Grace is a real sweet girl." His nose and mouth—his whole face really—screwed around the word *sweet*.

"You don't even know what we're talking about," Diana said.

"Yeah?" Ted said. "Well, let's keep it that way."

Allison's words echoed in Grace's head. *And Ted's real sweet*.

12

The television flickered silently in the corner. "Dad?" Grace reached to switch on the lamp, but Mr. Morrison let out three sharp snorts. She dropped her hand. He was asleep in his chair again. His head hung at an unnatural angle. She wanted to slide a pillow between his head and the chair, but the last time she'd tried that he'd jerked awake and glared at her. She went into the kitchen.

The new yellow enamel clock over the counter—her mom had brought it home last week to, she had said, *brighten the place up*—indicated five past seven. Even though the rest of them were rarely there on time—or at the same time—Mrs. Morrison always had the table set and ready at seven o' clock. Grace had always been there when she was little.

"Why don't you just let them get out their own plates?" Grace had asked. "When they come in?" It was sort of depressing, sitting around and eating dinner with the empty plates.

"We need to preserve some order," her mother had said, "despite what goes on in the rest of the world."

Or more to the point, Grace had come to realize over the years, despite what's going on in your own world. These days

Grace wasn't always on time herself, but it wasn't on purpose. School and work got in the way a lot. Mrs. Morrison might not realize it, but Grace appreciated order as much as she did.

Grace went into the hall and dropped her backpack at her bedroom door. The door to the stairway was open, and the stairwell light was on. A long, stuttering giggle erupted from the basement. Grace winced. Angela. She moved quietly to the top of the stairs.

"I still have that guy's ring somewhere." Sophie. "He was such a loser."

Grace sat down on the top step and leaned forward to listen.

"*He* was a loser? Look at that dress." Angela let loose the giggle again. "What were you going for? Scarlett O'Hara?"

"Hey"—Grace could hear the heavy photo album pages turning—"they didn't give us a lot to work with back then. Look at you."

"Oh." Angela sighed. "That was the military ball. I went with Kurt. I still have that dress."

"Kurt treated you like garbage." Sophie slapped through more pages. "Girls these days get up like super models."

"Ride in limousines."

"Have all the luck." Sophie laughed. "Where are Grace's pictures?"

Grace leaned in. "She doesn't have any," Angela said. "She doesn't go to dances. At least not formals."

More pages slapped down. "Nothing?" Sophie's voice was soft and oozing with pity.

Grace scooted back. Nothing, she thought. Exactly. No connection between her and those people whatsoever.

"Grace is different," Angela said.

Not just a different kind of person, Grace thought. She lived in a completely different world. Even if they were in the same house, at the same table, in the same conversation, they were always light-years apart.

"Different?" Sophie whispered.

Grace smiled.

"Oh." Angela jumped in. "I don't mean she's gay or anything."

Gay! Grace's mouth fell open. She dropped back onto the floor.

"Mom?" Sophie called up.

On cue, a key turned in the lock. Grace rolled over, jumped up, and ran down the hallway. Patty bounced through the front door. Mrs. Morrison followed. She gave two large pizza boxes to Grace. "Dinner," she said.

Sophie and Angela bubbled up out of the basement, whispering and giggling and touching.

Patty raced past Grace and hugged Angela's legs. "Mama!"

Sophie reached down, rustled the little girl's hair, and grinned at Mrs. Morrison. "How do you keep up with her?"

"Well." Mrs. Morrison's tone pushed like the sharp point of a pin into the light mood in the room. "You do what you have to do."

Angela's smile dissolved. She reached down and pulled Patty up into her arms.

Mrs. Morrison produced a sheath of forms and held them out to Sophie. "I picked up an application from the community college, and one from the technical school, and one from the new steak house on Crescent." She nodded. "They're still hiring."

"I just got here, Mother," Sophie said. "I'll get around to it."

Grace listened from the kitchen and nodded. So, she thought, Sophie was back to stay.

"I just picked up some forms," Mrs. Morrison said. "Just trying to help. You've got to start somewhere."

"Well, give me a freaking chance."

Grace heard her father thrashing around in the chair. The television blared. He must have hit the remote. Grace stacked the pizza boxes in the middle of the table and dealt plates around them.

"Sophie, you're thirty years old." Mrs. Morrison dropped her bag beside the armchair.

"Exactly," Sophie said.

Grace opened the refrigerator and pulled out a bag of greens and a cucumber.

"You had a few chances, don't you think," Mrs. Morrison said from the kitchen doorway. She turned and sank into the closest chair. Her husband wheeled in and parked beside her.

"I thought I'd make a salad," Grace said.

"Yes." Mrs. Morrison smiled. "That'll make it a real meal." She stood up and took a tomato off the windowsill.

Grace shook her head. "Sit down," she said. "I'll do it." She caught the caustic look Sophie threw her from the doorway.

Mrs. Morrison nodded, took two bottles of salad dressing from the refrigerator, and sat down. She held her hand out to Patty and helped her climb up into the seat beside her. She opened up the top pizza box and pulled out a slice of pepperoni for the little girl. From the one below it, she pulled out mushroom slices for herself and her husband. She smiled at him as she cut the slice into smaller, more manageable pieces.

Grace set the salad on the table and pulled out her chair. Angela and Sophie were still huddled and yammering in the doorway. "All I'm saying," Angela said, "is you have to watch your language around my kid."

Sophie expelled an impatient puff of air. Angela crashed down at the table, shuffled the pizza boxes—making it clear that neither of the toppings would have been her first choice—and knocked over the Parmesan shaker. Sophie reached over her shoulder, pulled up a slice of pepperoni, and ignored the plate her mother held out to her. She balanced the slice on her hand, glared back and forth between her mother and Angela, and chewed loudly.

Mrs. Morrison cocked her head at the salad bowl. "Grace made salad," she said.

"Good for Grace," Sophie said.

Mr. Morrison managed his pizza bits well enough, but he kept his eyes averted into the living room. Sometimes Grace wondered if her father's stroke was like a long, overdue vacation. In a way, he still set the tone. All of them, even Patty, finished up in silence.

After dinner, Grace put away the salad, since, basically, she was the only one who'd eaten any, but left the rest of the cleanup to somebody else. She took the phone out of its cradle in the kitchen and took it into her room. She closed the door and spread her books and papers over the bed.

First she called Diana. Her questions were now of the how-are-you-going-to-pull-this-off? variety rather than the are-you-nuts? sort. Grace provided the scant answers she had and jotted down a to-do list, Hannah-style, in response to the others.

"Who exactly," Diana finally asked, "is coming to this party?"

Grace laughed. "You want to be in charge of people?"

"Well," Diana said, "at least we know all the drama people love her."

Grace scrawled "Drama People" under the names "Diana, Tara, Ted?" In the right corner of her paper, she wrote "Sue." "First thing I've got to do"—she wrote "House"—"is talk to Sue about having a party in her house." She drew an arrow between *Sue* and *House*.

"Well, if we can't, we can always come up with someplace else."

"No!" Grace took a breath. "No," she said. "Allison's house would be the best place." The house was the only clear and certain object that connected all this talk to any possible reality. That, she supposed, and the fact that Diana was now, sort of, in the loop.

Grace was hunched over her lab sheets when Patty exploded through the door. "Bye-bye, Grace." She clawed at the bedspread. "Going home."

Grace pulled her up on the bed and hugged her. "Going home?" she said. "What do you want to do that for?"

Patty shook her head. "I don't."

Angela stood in the door and held out her arms. "Come on." Patty hopped to her mother. Angela caught her and nodded at Grace. "See you later."

Grace nodded back. She never took particular notice of Angela's comings and goings. She finished up the last problem on her lab sheet and called her lab partner, Sammy Thompson. She tightened up to prepare herself for the loud woman who always answered the phone. Grace wondered if she was his mother or grandmother or sister or crazy aunt or what, but was never rude enough to ask. The woman, and what sounded like a whole crowd, stayed loud in the background, same as every time she called.

"Yeah," Grace said. "I just wanted to make sure we got the same results on six and seven." They were supposed to have finished the questions in lab today, but Sammy was always wandering around and talking to all the other tables. Grace could never remember him writing down anything that actually came out of his own head. Of course, Ms. Mack didn't seem to mind what they put down, just as long as it was the same answer as their partner's. Ms. Mack was a real stickler for *concurrence*, as she called it.

"Oh," Sammy said. "What did you get?"

Grace read her answers slowly so he could write them down.

"Yeah," he said. "Sounds right."

"Yeah," Grace said, and hung up.

Sophie and her mother were still talking out in the living room. Grace read a couple of pages of social studies before falling back against her pillow. She couldn't understand their words, but their voices had an intense back-and-forth rhythm. She slung out her arms and closed her eyes. Listening to them was like sleeping in a motel room at the beach, with the balcony door open, hearing the constant lapping of the ocean waves.

"That's still your answer?" Mrs. Morrison's words rose like a wall and stopped the tide. "To just run away?"

Grace's eyes snapped open. She propped up on her elbows.

"Why do you care?" Sophie stormed back at her mother. "You didn't care then. You just sat there with your brand-new little baby and said, 'Go on then. I screwed you up, but I got another chance now.'"

Grace strained to hear something in the silence.

Finally, her mother spoke. "I never said anything like that."

Grace heard the jangle of keys. "Well," Sophie said. "That's what I heard." The front door opened. "Why else would a forty-five-year-old woman have a baby?" The door slammed. Sophie's car screamed down the driveway.

Grace quickly and quietly moved her books and papers off her bed. The silence scared her. She turned off the light, crept to the door, and cracked it. She heard the murmur of the television. Finally, a loud sigh. Good, Grace thought, she's alive. Grace slid under the covers and tried to see her mother holding her in her arms like that. She touched her cheek and grinned. Sophie had been talking about her. Grace had been the little baby.

She closed her eyes. She wished she could actually remember it. Being utterly helpless. Utterly innocent. She turned over on her side and pulled her knees up to her stomach. Utterly blameless.

Her father clattered past her bedroom door. Her mother followed along behind him. "I never said anything like that," Mrs. Morrison muttered. "She never gave me a chance."

Grace rolled over. She'd never really had a chance to be that perfect little baby. Sophie had blamed her from the very beginning. *Tautology*, she thought.

13

So," Kennedy said for the third time. "Coefficients."

Grace kneaded her palm into her cheek.

"Wake up!" Kennedy always opened class with the assumption that they were all asleep. Then she'd roll right into her math's-not-nearly-as-bad-as-all-of-you-think spiel. And all of her lessons were punctuated with allowances for "those of you with visual, spatial, auditory, linear"—her categories were never ending—"learning disorders."

Today, like every day, Grace sat through fifth period clenched against Kennedy's clichés. Tyrone winked at Grace, and she smiled at him. If it wasn't for the brilliant distraction of Tyrone's sideshow, Kennedy would have already driven her completely insane.

Tyrone held up the blank pages of his fat notebook and fanned them again. Kennedy cut her bright green eyes at him. Those unnatural contact lenses constantly tortured Kennedy to near tears. Grace wondered what color her eyes really were. Maybe something even more unnatural. Maybe no color at all. Kennedy screwed on her smile and reiterated, "Coefficients are those friendly, recognizable numbers you see in the equation."

Grace dropped her head down, but jerked it to a halt just before impact. She slid the Japanese alphabet out from under her notebook and made the first two strokes of the *Zo*. She mouthed the sound. The look of the characters came more easily to her than the sound. Maybe, Grace thought, she actually did have one of those *auditory disabilities*.

Tyrone fanned his paper again. Kennedy dropped her hand from the board. "Clear your desks," she said.

The class shifted to attention. "Everything?" "Our books?" "Paper?" "Notebooks?"

Ms. Kennedy gave one sharp nod to all their questions.

"We can't take notes?" That was from Tyrone. Brilliant.

"Just clear your desks"—Kennedy struggled to anchor that smile—"and listen."

Tyrone stretched out his legs and rested his head in the palm of his big hand. Kennedy lifted her hand up to the board and gave a weaker nod.

Grace shook her head. Tyrone forced her to banish books, paper, and note taking, and yet Kennedy still thought she'd won the battle.

"So," Kennedy said. "Coefficients."

Grace eased her hands into her lap, and, under the cover of the desktop, she began writing *Zo* carefully, onto her left hand with her right. She couldn't remember if there were two little strokes on the left and one on the right, or vice versa. She should have slid her stuff under her desk, rather than into her backpack. Then she could have just pulled out her alphabet sheet with her foot and double-checked it. She stared at her hand. Two on the right didn't look altogether wrong. More lightly, and smaller, on her wrist, she sketched it the other way. No, the first one was right. She looked up to see Kennedy passing out a quiz.

"You may," she said, looking directly at Tyrone, "take out a single sheet of paper."

Tyrone tore a page out of his notebook slowly, and, somehow, loudly.

Grace reached up to take the test with her right hand, but Kennedy's eyes lingered on her left one. Kennedy's lips parted as if she was about to speak, but she merely exhaled sharply and moved on down the aisle. Grace scanned the quiz. There was no mention of narrative sentences. She smiled and set to work.

Grace made it to sixth period first for a change, but Allison rushed in right behind her. She dropped her books, bent down, and gripped the edge of Grace's desk. "Did you talk to him?" she whispered.

Grace leaned away from her. "Who?" she asked.

Allison silently, but emphatically, pushed the name *Ted* through her purple lips.

"Oh." Grace shrugged. "Not yet."

"Think about it," Allison said. "It's too perfect to pass up."

Stubblefield rushed in and banged the class to attention. Allison flounced down into her seat.

"What about last night's reading?" Stubblefield said. "Pretty provocative stuff, huh?"

Grace folded her arms and sagged lower in her desk. Too

bad he came so late in the day. She wanted to listen to him. Her eyes drifted to the shiny blue shoe balancing on Allison's toes. It was bound to fall off.

Stubblefield tapped the board with his marker. Grace looked up and scrawled down his last couple of sentences. Allison yawned and stretched her arms over her head. Grace's eyes followed them up to the tips of her glittery blue nails. The Ted idea certainly was not perfect. At least not in the regular world. One giant step over into Allison Land, though, and it suddenly made a sort of sense.

"Grace." Stubblefield's voice pushed through to her.

She flinched. "What?"

All the kids were looking at her. He nodded at the short-haired office girl standing in the doorway. "You're wanted in the principal's office."

Grace sighed. She should have known the Saylers business wasn't finished. "Should I take my books?"

Stubblefield shrugged and looked at the office girl. She pushed her tortoiseshell glasses up on her nose and shrugged. Stubblefield nodded at Grace. "Perhaps you should."

Grace grabbed her backpack and headed out. Allison gave her a thumbs-up. Mr. Stubblefield said, "Happy trails." The office girl didn't say anything. She just turned around and led the way. As Grace followed, she checked the front pocket of her pack to make sure she had all of her evidence—the old schedules and papers. She did. She appreciated the opportunity to air the whole thing out before the principal. She'd tried to get an appointment with Ms. Jackson every day of that first screwy week but had been put off until it was too late to matter. Her father had always said, to solve a problem, you had to get to the top. "The real top," he had emphasized. "They'll lie to you in a heartbeat."

"How would you know if it's the real top then?" Somebody had asked. Not Grace. Most likely Angela. "If they always lie?"

"Because," her father had said, "you get action."

Angela might have asked the question, but Grace remembered the answer. Angela had probably forgotten the words before he'd even closed his mouth on the last one.

"Come in, Grace." Ms. Jackson was waiting at her office door. She glanced down around Grace's waist. Grace looked down, too, but she didn't see anything. "Have a seat."

Grace sat down. Ms. Jackson closed the door and sat down behind her desk. "I'm sorry to interrupt your class, Grace, but don't worry. You won't be marked absent."

Grace fumbled with her backpack, but Ms. Jackson stared at Grace's hands, so she stopped.

"Ms. Kennedy was just so anxious—"

Grace sat up straight. "Ms. Kennedy?" Grace's mind raced to the conclusion that Ms. Kennedy had finally realized Grace didn't belong in the friendly numbers group. She grinned. "She—?"

"Let me see your hands, Grace." Ms. Jackson held out both of her hands, palm up. Grace took the cue and laid her hands on top of them. Ms. Jackson sighed. "Educators," she said, "are trained to be on the alert for gang paraphernalia and symbols." She clasped both of Grace's hands. "We depend upon prevention," she said, "more than you might realize."

"Ma'am?" Grace said.

Ms. Jackson shook Grace's left hand. "What does this symbol mean, Grace?"

Grace blinked at Ms. Jackson. "Ms. Kennedy thinks I'm in a gang?" She had to dig through the big compartment of her backpack to find the copy of the Japanese alphabet to show Ms. Jackson. Apparently, Grace thought, she was going to have to start compiling a whole new packet of evidence, for a completely new and different defense.

14

sian gangs," Diana whispered into the phone, like that bright-eyed twit on Channel Six. "Today's threat to all you hold sacred." Her affected husky voice broke into a shower of giggles. Grace could hear her feet bang on the floor.

It was a pretty good story. Grace laughed, too. "I mean," she said, "just when you think you've got a grip"—she dropped back against the headboard—"they kick you from some completely new, whacked-out angle."

"But an *Asian* gang?"

Grace stretched her left arm up, flexed her hand, and smiled at the Zo. "Hey," she said. "They've got to go with the evidence."

"Evidence!" Diana laughed. "What a bunch of idiots."

"Ms. Jackson was okay, though," Grace said. "I showed her the sheet with the Japanese alphabet and told her that I knew it was pretty childish to be writing on my hand—"

"What did she say about Kennedy?"

"Nothing really." A key turned in the front door. Grace scooted to the edge of the bed, stretched out her leg, and, with her foot, closed her bedroom door. "They all stick together."

She laughed. "But right off I could tell she thought it was totally nutty."

Sophie flung open the door and blurted, "Where's Mom and Dad?"

Grace straightened up. "Physical therapy." She noticed that Sophie was wearing a dress for the first time since she'd been back. Up until now her uniform had been a tank top and jeans. Into the phone, Grace said, "What?"

Sophie lazily surveyed Grace's room. "What time do they get back?"

"Six-thirty or so."

"So it ended okay?" Diana asked.

"Yeah." Grace hunched back down into her conversation. "You know these *educators*. They've got to make you into some kind of problem, right?"

"That only they can solve."

"Exactly," Grace said. "So if I wasn't a gang member, a *discipline* problem, then I had to be an *academic* problem. She had to provide the proper instruction."

Sophie had gone out into the hall, but she backed up and stared at Grace for a moment before moving on. Grace scooted over and extended her leg to shut the door again, but she thought better of it. Sophie might take it the wrong way, and Grace wasn't like Angela. She wasn't familiar enough with Sophie to fall into the insults right away. She pulled her leg back onto the bed. "She went off into this spiel about Ridgewood and Pace—"

"The private schools?"

Grace nodded. "And about how Japanese was supposed to come in when they brought in German, but"—she shook her head—"then she rambled off something about the superintendent, which she said she shouldn't be telling me—"

"What?" Diana asked. "Shouldn't be telling you what?"

"I don't know. I didn't get it. But, anyway, she said she might be able to work out a Japanese class for me, and I told her I didn't want to be taking any more classes—"

"Why not?" Diana said. "Maybe a Japanese class would be good."

"I don't want school taking over every single thing in my life." Diana, she thought, ought to be able to remember why not. "I told her if she really wanted to do something for me, she could put me in a decent math class."

Diana hooted. "No," she said. "Really?"

"Well, I didn't say exactly that. I made on like I was the problem, not Kennedy."

"Well, yeah."

"And you know the big rule they spew? About how your schedule can't be changed after the first ten days, blah, blah, blah."

"Yeah?"

"Well, if Ms. Jackson has ever heard of it, she didn't let on."

"They make 'em, they break 'em."

"So, long story short, she set up this placement test Friday afternoon. With that Mr. Frankel you were telling me about."

"Wow, Grace," Diana said. "That was really, really great."

Grace slumped back on her pillows. "But now," she said, "I've got to take the test. What if I blow it? Kennedy would totally own me."

"This is too perfect," Diana said. "My mom just bought this

math workbook for me. This geometry/algebra overview. It's got everything."

Perfect, Allison echoed in Grace's head. Ms. Kaye said that the English language was huge, that it had twice as many words as German, but everyone kept shooting the same old ones at Grace. Not that she was any better. She shot them right back.

"Come get it right now," Diana said.

"Don't you need it?"

"No way." Diana laughed. "I want it out of the house."

"Tomorrow then," Grace said. "Nobody's here. I don't have a ride."

"I'm here." Grace looked up and saw Sophie standing in the doorway. She'd changed back into her jeans. "Where do you want to go?" She jangled her keys on her finger.

Sophie pulled up in front of Diana's house, turned off the ignition, and bolted out of the car.

Grace scrambled to keep up with her. "What are you doing?" Grace asked. "I'm just here to pick up a book."

Sophie walked right up to the door and rang the doorbell. "Got to get the word out," she said. "Sophie's back in town."

Diana's mother opened the door. "Hello." She frowned for an instant but erupted into a smile when she saw Grace. She touched Sophie's arm. "Why, you're Grace's sister!" She pulled Sophie inside. "How could I miss that?"

"I came to borrow a book—"

"Diana!" Kate called out. "Grace is here." She nodded toward the dining room. "Have a seat," she said. "Can I get you anything to drink?"

Sophie plopped right down. Grace glared at her sister. "No, thank you," she said. The smells of dinner cooking wafted out of the kitchen. This was ridiculous, she thought. Plain rude. Grace alone didn't matter—she was like furniture around here—but showing up with her sister right at dinnertime was just wrong.

"So," Kate said, "you live in California."

"I did," Sophie said softly.

"So you're back for good."

"I suppose I am."

Mission accomplished, Grace thought. Word's out. Sophie's back.

"I lived in northern California for a couple of years after college, before Tony and I were married," Kate said. "I liked it."

Sophie nodded. "I liked it, too." She smiled. "But I really screwed up out there."

Grace leaned forward. She was willing to be embarrassed in front of Kate if it meant gathering a little more information.

Diana interrupted from the doorway. "What are you doing out here?" She saw Sophie. "Oh." She sat down and asked. "Do you remember me?"

Sophie wiggled her fingers overhead. "Little girl with the crazy hair, right?"

The kitchen door slammed, and someone began banging away in the kitchen.

Diana pushed back her curls. "What gave me away?" She looked at her mother. "So did Grace tell you what happened?"

Kate shook her head. Diana launched into the Asian gang

story. Ted slid in from the kitchen and leaned against the wall to listen. Ted and Sophie laughed. Diana slapped the table.

Kate smiled. "Poor Grace," Kate said. "It's a tough system."

"Oh," Diana said. "I told Mom about Allison's party."

"It's a lovely idea, Grace." Kate looked at Diana. "It's got to be tough being new at school."

Diana laughed. "Mom, I think Allison does okay."

Ted laughed. "Poor little rich girl," he said.

So, Grace thought, at least he knows who she is.

"Allison?" Sophie flexed her fingers. "With the fingernails?"

Diana nodded. "And Mom said we could have it here if we had to."

"No," Grace said. "I just need to talk to Sue."

Ted straightened up and folded his arms. "Are you kidding me?" he said. "I have to lay down and beg to have a couple of guys over, and you're just going to up and throw a party here for some . . . girl?" He shook his head and walked out the other door.

Kate and Sophie drifted into some old California memory. The front door opened and closed. Tony peeked in, said, "Hello, ladies," and disappeared down the hall.

A buzzer went off in the kitchen. Kate looked over her shoulder. "You two can stay for dinner, right?"

Grace stood up. "No," she said. "We've got dinner waiting at home."

Kate stood up. "Well, come into the kitchen with me, Sophie, and I'll get those numbers." She'd said she knew a couple of people Sophie should call about a job.

Diana headed back to her room to get the math book. Grace

was following her but ducked into the big room where Ted was stretched out on the couch watching television.

"Don't worry," she said. "The party's not going to be here."

He shrugged. "I don't care." He reached up and took Grace's hand. "This what caused all the commotion?"

Grace looked at the *Zo* and nodded.

"Won't it wash off?"

"I guess," Grace said.

Ted grinned. "Uh huh." He squeezed her fingers. "Poor Grace."

15

Low metal fixtures hung over every booth in the restaurant. Every second one was lit. Sophie chose a dark one. "So"—she squinted across the table at Grace—"what's bugging you?"

Grace looked at her watch. "We ought to call Mom."

"I left her a note." Sophie studied Grace's face. "I just missed your birthday, didn't I?"

Grace shrugged. That one, she thought, and every one that came before it. She suddenly recalled how it was right around her birthday every year that her mother called Sophie—or at least made a real effort to track her down. "Is your birthday in September, too?"

Sophie nodded. "The fifteenth."

Grace's was September 12. "Only three days apart." Grace looked at her sister. Sophie had probably blamed her for that, too. Screwing up her birthday.

"Three days and sixteen years." Sophie squinted. "Doesn't Mom let you drive the car? You can borrow mine sometime."

"I don't have my license."

"Why not?"

"If you're under eighteen, a parent has to be with you, and, you know, Mom's never got any time."

"Mmm hmm." Sophie drew a long sip from her mug. "I could take you." She wiggled up straight and cocked her head. "I could be your mother. Just barely, but still I could."

Grace did the math. Just barely, maybe. In Sophie's world. "I think they check," she said.

Sophie snapped her fingers. "You got to just go for it. Nine times out of ten, you get away with it."

Grace nodded. Maybe it would work. When it came to breaking rules, at least Sophie had experience.

"You graduate next year?"

Sophie apparently didn't have the time for Grace to think one thing through before she jumped on to the next thing. Grace turned off her brain and jumped, too. "Two more years. I'm a sophomore."

"If I'd stuck it out, I'd have graduated when I was seventeen." Sophie grinned. "Guess that means I'm smarter than you."

Grace gripped the edge of the table and leaned into Sophie. "No," she said. "All it means is that you and I have *inconvenient* birthdays. Mom had the choice to start us early or late. She went the early road with you."

Sophie leaned back. "Worked for me."

Grace's mouth dropped open. "No." She shook her head. "It didn't."

Sophie stuck out the index finger on her left hand. "I'm here." Then the one on her right hand. "I'm alive." She presented her open palms. "What more do you want?"

"To graduate, maybe?" Grace leaned closer. "The way Mom

saw it, she put you in the first grade before your sixth birthday, then ten years later you drop out, run away, and totally screw up. So, with me, she did the opposite. I had to wait one whole year, until I was almost seven, to start first grade." She jabbed her finger at Sophie. "You screw up, Angela screws up, I get screwed." Grace fell back against her seat. "Story of my life."

Sophie threw up her hands. "Okay, okay, okay," she said. "Mom said you were listening. Said I had to apologize." She pushed her lips up into a phony little smile. "Sorry."

The waitress set the pizza on the table.

"You're not supposed to take it personally," Sophie said. The waitress set down her second beer and Grace's second Coke. Sophie looked up at the waitress and said, "Thanks." She nodded at Grace. "So sorry, okay."

Grace lifted a piece of pizza and laid it on her plate. "What," she said, "are you talking about?"

"You know," Sophie said, "when I went off on Mom, blaming all my *youthful indiscretions* on"—she smiled and pointed at Grace—"the baby." She shook her head. "Please." She pulled a slice for herself from the pan. She didn't bother to disconnect the strands; she just took whatever cheese came with it to her plate. "I hardly knew you were there." She held up her thumb and forefinger, indicating about an inch and a half. "You were about this big."

"That," Grace said, "makes me feel so much better."

Sophie took a big bite and downed half her beer. She looked past Grace, as if she were trying to focus on something faraway. "The story of my life"—she patted her chest—"began a hell of a long time before you came along." She pointed at Grace. "You were just a thing that happened one day."

"Even better," Grace said.

Sophie picked up her mug and drained it. She held up her finger. "We need a box," she told the waitress. To Grace, she said, "Do you have any money?"

Grace unfolded her arms, lifted up, and slid six crumpled one-dollar bills out of her jeans pocket. She found four quarters in her purse. "Seven dollars," she said.

Sophie counted the bills in her wallet. "That's good," she said.

"What if I didn't have any money?" Grace asked.

Sophie waved her away. "Like I said, nine times out of ten, it all works out."

When they got out to the car, Sophie stooped halfway in, then said, "You want to drive?"

Grace shook her head, but she couldn't help herself. "Yeah." She circled around the front of the car. Sophie circled around the back. Grace slid behind the wheel and adjusted the mirror. It was loose, though, so it slid back down. They traveled a couple of blocks in silence, for which Grace was grateful. She didn't have a lot of experience driving at night.

"You really ought to get your license," Sophie said. "You're ready." She pointed to the right. "Pull in here."

Grace turned into the parking lot of a strip shopping center. Sophie arched up and pulled three dollars out of her left pocket. Grace realized they hadn't been cutting it as close at the restaurant as she had thought. Sophie rummaged in the ashtray for quarters and dimes. "Now that I think about it," she said, "I only meant to leave Mom a note. I didn't actually do it." She grinned. "Maybe some ice cream will put her in a good mood."

Grace waited in the car. They were going to have to listen to their mother complain for no reason at all. They could have called from the restaurant.

Sophie hopped back in. "Pralines and cream." She spread her fingers. "Maybe I should hire that Allison to do my nails."

"She's rich," Grace said. "She doesn't need your money."

Sophie nodded. "Flashy and rich." She laughed. "Better make that a damn good party."

Grace turned onto Campbellton Road. The car was back in the driveway. "Mom's going to be so mad," she said.

Sophie touched Grace's arm. "Don't worry," she said. "I'm here to take the heat in person now." She patted her gently and pulled away. "No need to suffer for the sins of your sister any longer."

Mrs. Morrison informed them that she had been worried, and that she was angry. Grace was surprised, however, to see that the ice cream actually did make a difference. She would have thought such a stupid and obvious gesture would be insulting, but Sophie and her mother settled back peacefully with big bowlfuls and watched television.

Grace took hers into her bedroom and closed the door. She read the first section of Diana's math book, where they gave you test-taking tips, then went on to a couple of practice exercises. She had forgotten a lot of stuff.

She lay down and rolled over on her stomach. She'd felt a little uneasy at first, talking to so many people at one time about this bogus party. They did all seem to enjoy the idea, though, which only confirmed what Allison had said. Grace reached over, turned off the lamp, and kicked the math book onto the floor.

Right before Grace fell asleep, when her brain had just begun to swim away in the dreamy darkness, Sophie banged through the door and blinded her with the overhead light. "Look at this," Sophie said. Grace pushed up on her elbows and blinked.

Sophie shot out her right arm and unfurled something black and red and green and fabulous. "I used to wear it as a robe," Sophie said, "but it's silk. It would look great over black pants or something."

Grace sat up. "What?"

"It's genuine Japanese." Sophie smoothed it over her arm and sat down on the bed. She pulled up her legs and crossed them. "What do they call it?"

"A kimono?" Grace said.

"Yeah, yeah." Sophie nodded. "Like I said, we used to wear them as robes, but—"

"We?" Grace wrinkled up her nose. "Who?"

Sophie shook her head. "It's clean," she said. "It just wrinkles easily." She lowered her lashes and sighed. "They were a nice bunch of girls." She laughed. "They gave me a surprise party."

Grace squinted at her. "Really?"

Sophie nodded. "It was at this club up north, and I just could not take it another day, so I told them I was pregnant—"

"Pregnant?"

Sophie held up her hand. "Stop the presses," she said. "I wasn't." She laughed. "I admit I knew they'd take up a collection or something, but those girls threw me a baby shower." She threw out her arms. "Surprise!" Sophie leaned against the headboard and smiled. "The next day I went around to the mall, returned all the gifts for cash, and got the hell out of that town."

"Huh?"

Sophie shrugged. "They would have taken up that money in a collection anyway." She stood up. "This way, they had a good time doing it."

Grace nodded. Sophie turned off the light and closed her door, but the dreamy darkness was gone.

16

The skinny boy hugged the corridor wall. He rolled the receiver on his temple. "But how come?" he whined.

Grace was sorry to push in so close to his agony, but she stood firm. It was tough to get the pay phone at lunch. You could either care or maintain position. Not both.

"But how come, Bunny?" he asked. "It doesn't make any sense." He sniffed. "How can you just not like me anymore?"

Grace exhaled loud and hard. She threw her sympathy wholeheartedly to Bunny. How could she have ever liked him, Grace thought. That was the question. She shifted the books cradled in her right arm to her left.

The boy rolled away from Grace. "Well, what if I was to call up your mother right now? And what if I was to tell her Little Miss Perfect's not even at school." He slammed the receiver down so hard it bounced out and knocked against the wall. "How about that, huh?" His pale eyes flitted around Grace, as if he expected her to answer.

Grace grabbed the receiver and dropped in her coins.

The boy gave her the hateful look he was probably afraid to give his girlfriend. Grace was happy to return it for her. He walked away muttering. Grace punched in Allison's number. It rang four times. Allison had said Sue would be home for lunch today. Two girls pushed up behind Grace and waited. She glanced over her shoulder. No one she knew.

On the sixth ring, Sue picked up. "Hello."

"Ms. Anderson," Grace said. "This is Grace Morrison." She cleared her throat. "I go to school with Allison."

"Of course, Grace," Sue said.

"I was wondering," Grace started. "Diana and I . . . We . . ." She shouldn't drag Diana into it. "I'd like to give Allison a birthday party, a surprise party, ah . . . on her birthday, that Saturday night, at your house."

Sue's silence went way too long. Then, when she did start talking, she stumbled. Sue's manner was usually distinctly quick and sharp. "If only Dennis didn't have to be out of town that night." Sue picked up the pace. "He's got to be in Greenville that day, and then I have a meeting in the evening."

Grace nodded. It was over. "Oh, well."

"I'd blow it off if I could, but I can't, and it'll go late." She sighed. "It's not that I don't trust you, and I know you don't want us around anyway—"

"No, ma'am," Grace said. She was fairly certain that was the wrong thing to say. Sue was confusing her.

"But a house full of kids," she said. "That's a lot of parents for me to answer to."

If Sue was going back to work, Grace thought, she was probably making this call from the breakfast nook, looking out through the lace curtains. If she was home for the day she might be sitting cross-legged on the daybed back in the green room. She tuned back in to Sue mid-sentence.

". . . going shopping and then meeting Dennis for dinner on Friday, but this would be so good for her." Sue took a breath.

Grace was lost. The conversation had clearly taken a hard turn. "Well . . . ," she said.

"It's what she wanted all along. A party. But it just wasn't a good time." Sue was tapping something. A pencil, Grace thought. Or a pen. Maybe she was sitting at the table. "We said she could do something over the holidays, but that wasn't good enough. She said, 'Then it wouldn't be my birthday.' You wouldn't know it to look at her, but she is very traditional." She laughed. "I don't know where she gets it."

Listening didn't help Grace grasp the gist any better. "So . . . ?" One way or another, this part had to be settled today.

"I tell you what," Sue said. "I'll run it by Dennis and get back to you. Will you be home this afternoon?"

"I'll be at work. At the Art Center."

"Downtown? Where Allison took her acting classes?"

"Yes, ma'am," Grace said. "You can call me there."

"Thank you, Grace," Sue said. "Thank you so much."

Grace hung up. The girl behind her pushed in and grabbed the receiver. Instead of tracking down Tara as she'd planned, Grace bought an ice cream sandwich and sat down on the floor in the corridor outside the office. Watching Allison mess with Sue and Dennis could be entertaining, but she didn't enjoy actually being a part of it. She finished up the ice cream, leaned her head against the wall, and closed her eyes until lunch was over.

Grace sat in math and transported herself into the nook and the green room. It had been an absurd idea from the beginning, but she'd come to believe in Allison's power to make things be. She was embarrassed by her disappointment.

"Tyrone," Ms. Kennedy said, "I have no power over the thermostat."

Grace glanced over at Tyrone; his arms were wrapped tight, and he was shivering and chattering. Grace smiled. Now he was too cold.

Grace parked her left elbow on the desk and twisted her hand in the air. The *Zo* was faint but visible. She leaned in and pressed her left cheek into her palm, careful to keep the hand angled so that the character was always in Kennedy's line of vision. Grace hadn't expected the teacher to apologize exactly, but she had expected her to say something.

I will not, Grace promised herself, blow that test on Friday. She glared at Kennedy. She would not give her the satisfaction.

17

All the framed art was hung. Hannah had saved the 3-D exhibits for Grace. "Okay." Grace pointed to opposite corners. "Like last time?"

Hannah sighed. "Keep the traffic patterns in mind."

Grace nodded. Hannah worried herself sick over pottery. It was something she couldn't control. "You see how people sling their arms around," Hannah had said. "Pottery breaks." Grace walked a wooden stand down the hall and thought about why she was put in charge of this most fragile operation. If a piece was broken, it could, sort of, be Grace's fault. At least more Grace's fault than Hannah's.

"I warned her," Hannah could say, "about the traffic patterns." No. Grace shook that accusation out of her head. Hannah wasn't like that.

Grace went back down the hall to get the taller companion stand. She hugged it and walked it down the hall, checking every once in a while to make sure she wasn't marking up the floor. The stand wasn't all that heavy. She could have carried it, except that it was impossible to get a real grip on it.

"What are you doing here?"

Grace stopped and turned around. Diana wrinkled her nose and rubbed at it with her fist. "I'm working," Grace said.

Diana wiped her hands on her clay-stained apron. "What time is it?"

"Three," Grace said. "A little past."

"Oh, man." Diana shook her head. "My mom's already home, and I promised her I'd do this writing thing she wanted me to do." She shrugged and motioned Grace into the studio. A tall vase with squared edges rose from the table.

Grace ran her finger down its smooth, deep blue side. "It's beautiful," she said.

Diana pointed to the gray, half-constructed slabs beside it. "I'm doing a shorter version, and I was thinking about putting a hole in the bottom and wiring it up as a lamp." She looked at Grace. "What do you think?"

"Well," Grace said. "Yeah."

Diana nodded. The collected curls on the top of her head jumped around. "I know," she said. "Too interior decorator, right?"

Grace shook her head. "No, but"—she looked back at the vase—"would you just buy a lamp shade or what?"

"No." Diana slapped her hands together and clay dust puffed out. "That's the best part. Susan"—she cocked her head—"you know, the tole lady."

Grace nodded. "And calligraphy." Wednesdays, seven to nine. Her classes always filled up right away.

"Yeah," Diana said. "And she paints lamp shades." She leaned in and gently pressed the seams of the slabs. "She showed me some. They were cool."

"That sounds good then," Grace said. "It just seemed a

shame to make something like this, and then top it off with a regular old lamp shade."

The slabs separated and fell apart. Diana stuck out her tongue. "I knew it," she said. "Too wet." She sat down and straightened out the pieces. "And tomorrow it'll be too dry."

A voice called out from the glaze room. "Not if you wrap them in plastic and vent just one side."

Grace looked around. "Who's that?" she whispered.

Diana shrugged. "This old lady who comes in every morning." She pointed at a gargoyle on the top shelf. "That's one of hers."

Grace returned the demon's hard gaze.

"She's real nice." Diana carefully transferred one of the slabs to a board. "I'll come out and help you as soon as I clean up."

Grace nodded and moved toward the door. "Oh, yeah," she said. "I talked to Sue. The party's probably off."

"Why?"

"Well, she and Dennis can't be there, and she wasn't too thrilled with the idea of turning her house over to us."

"Well, my mom did say we could do it at our house, if we had to. . . ."

Grace shook her head. "No. I say we just forget it."

Diana slid another slab onto the board. "I've already mentioned it to some people here—you know, from that workshop she did in the summer."

"I'll tell them it's off." Grace moved to the door. "I've got to get those other stands to the lobby." The last four moved more quickly, now that she had her method and rhythm. The box of fabric she took into Hannah's office to press.

Hannah held up her hand. "I was thinking that we might just leave them bare."

"Maybe," Grace said. Recently Hannah had begun preaching a clean, uncluttered, less-is-more philosophy. Several pieces of furniture had, in her words, "fallen away" from her apartment, and today she was dressed in a black T-shirt and jeans instead of one of her gypsy outfits. It followed, of course, that the concept would extend to the Center. Grace lifted one of the sculptures out of the box from behind Hannah's desk, took it out, and set it on a bare wooden stand.

Hannah followed her out. She shook her head. "Use the drapes, but remember—"

"Less is more?"

Hannah smiled. "Exactly." She lifted the sculpture off the stand. "I trust your judgment."

Grace watched Hannah glide back into her office. Her spare new style made her appear stronger. The gypsy clothes were very cool on their own, but Grace could see now how they had swallowed up Hannah's body. The front door rattled open, and Grace turned around.

Sue clicked up to Grace in her black pumps and grabbed her hands. "Grace, I am so, so sorry, but with everything that's going on right now, we just don't see our way clear—" She let go and held up her hands. "The truth is, I was in your corner all along, but her father . . ." She sighed. "Well, Dennis is a lawyer. Can't win with him. But I do thank you"—she glanced over to the hall—"and you, Diana."

Diana stared speechless. Grace shook her head. "It was just an idea," she said.

Sue clasped her hands together as if she were about to pray.

"Oh, no, no, no." Sue shook her head. "It was a supremely considerate and thoughtful idea, and just what Allison needs. We worry about her constantly, and to know she has friends like you, well . . ." She exhaled loudly.

Grace blushed. The room went very hot. She just wanted Sue to leave and all this to be over. Instinctively, she looked over her shoulder. Just as she expected, Hannah stood in the doorway and watched.

Sue stopped and looked, too. "I'm sorry," she said to Hannah. "This is a place of business, and here I am—"

"Do I know you?" Hannah asked.

"I . . ." Sue clasped her hands. A professional calm settled over her. "My daughter, Allison, took some classes here this summer."

"Sue?"

Sue took a step back. "Hannah?" She clapped her hands together. "Oh, my god!"

Sue's pumps clicked across the floor. Hannah put her arm around her shoulder, led her into her office and, once again, closed the door.

Diana looked at Grace and laughed. "What," she whispered, "was that?"

"I have no idea."

Diana sat down at Grace's desk, called her mother, and tried to explain how she'd lost track of time. Grace grinned. Kate might be mad at Diana now, she thought, but as soon as she saw the vase, she'd get over it. Kate had always been a real sucker for art and creativity.

Grace experimented with the displays. She draped a blue piece of cloth over one stand and a yellow piece over the one beside it. She stepped back, then moved in and placed a yellow over the blue. Diana, who was still on the phone pleading her case, gave a thumbs-up to that idea, but there weren't enough pieces to make it work. Grace went back to her original plan.

Sue burst out of Hannah's office. She waved her arms over her head. "Party on, girls."

Hannah nodded. "Seems it was only a chaperone problem," she said. "And I can do that." She touched Sue's shoulder. "Don't worry," she said, "I'll bring backup."

"I'd love to meet him." Sue looked at her watch, then back at Hannah. "I'll call you later." She nodded. "Thank you, girls." She clicked out the way she'd clicked in.

Grace and Diana turned to Hannah. "We knew each other," she said, "in another life."

Diana shook her head. "Another life?"

Hannah laughed. "In college. Sort of. She and Dennis actually went to Chapel Hill, but my roommate at Duke, Annie, was good friends with them, so they came up a time or two." She shrugged. "What are the odds?"

"Really." Diana stood up. "What are the odds?"

Hannah studied Grace. "Sue said this party was your idea." She raised her eyebrows. "Now, what, I'd like to know, are the odds of that?"

18

All the kids except Allison were hunched over their objects and shuffling through their index cards. Allison slouched out long into the aisle and fluttered her lashes. She was dressed, oddly, the same as many of the other kids. Her nylon pants, which matched her jacket, were unzipped over her cross-trainers. Her hair was folded up into a wispy fan and fastened with a common plastic clasp.

Grace slid into her desk. Allison screwed around to face her. "Where's your tree?" she asked.

Grace cocked her head toward the front of the room. The bonsai was sitting behind Stubblefield's desk. Sophie had given her a ride in this morning—had actually let Grace drive—in order to drop it off. "He won't get to me until Monday anyway."

"I don't know," Allison said. "Nikki's not here."

Grace glanced over to the row of desks beside the wall. Nikki *Hand*.

"She wasn't at lunch either, so . . . ." Allison shook her head.

Grace shrugged. "Whatever."

Stubblefield rapped his desk. "Okay, people."

Allison's speech was great. Her outfit was her object from another culture. She held out her arms. "The product of the labor of little Chinese children, little Thai children, little Filipino children, working twenty-hour days for slave wages." She turned around. "What they make in a week, you wouldn't bother to stoop down and pick up off the sidewalk."

Her eyes settled on Randy Waters. He wiggled up and looked around. "Twenty hours?" He shook his head.

Allison loped by him and slid into her seat. Grace heard muttering up and down the aisles about how she didn't really do the assignment and how it shouldn't count. What a bunch of morons, Grace thought. She crossed them all off the guest list. After the next report, they seemed to be over it, but then that only made them bigger morons. Grace ran her eyes up and down the rows of desks. Maybe Lyndon, she thought. Or Charlie. Grace wasn't too worried about people anyway. At least not in terms of bodies. There was Diana's bunch, and Tara had pretty much guaranteed the Drama Club, except for four or five kids who were going to Charlotte for a concert.

Nikki's absence did screw up the order, and then Kathy took the one-letter-grade hit to put her speech off until Monday. Grace's name came up with thirteen minutes left on the clock, which seemed like enough time to deliver a five- to seven-minute presentation, but even Stubblefield considered cutting them off right there. He looked at his roll book, looked at the clock, tapped his pencil on his desk, then looked at the class and said, "Okay, Grace. You're up."

Grace set the bonsai on Stubblefield's desk, shifting it around so that it wouldn't obscure his face. The kids laughed, and even though it was more at Stubblefield's expressions and gyrations than at anything Grace had done, it worked. Ms. Kaye always recommended an icebreaker when they spoke in front of English class. Then, when Grace went on to say that *bonsai* was Japanese for "tree in a pot," they laughed again.

Beside the bonsai itself, Grace had the picture that her mother had taken of her father holding the juniper just after he dug it up. She gave it to a girl in the front row to pass around. She held up the scissors and little saw she used for trimming. The photo and tools would have been enough to get an A out of Stubblefield—he was mad for visual aids— but she also had a literary reference. She closed with the folktale about how, to show his hospitality, a poor old man had burned his priceless bonsai collection to warm a visiting nobleman.

"What an idiot," Randy Waters said.

"Indeed," Stubblefield muttered.

Grace smiled. She knew what he meant.

When she was done, Stubblefield asked his perfunctory questions. "How long have you had this object?" and "When were you first aware of its cultural significance?" The tone sounded. A girl up front leaned over and put the photo on Stubblefield's desk. Everyone shifted one way or another at the same time. Stubblefield sighed. "Dismissed," he said. He picked up the photo and studied it.

Allison touched Grace's arm. "How's it going?"

Grace smiled. "What?" she asked. She had decided to pretend, from now on, that the party actually was a surprise. "That way," she had told Allison, "you'll have as much fun as everyone else."

Allison nodded. "Fine," she said. "You got that math thing today?"

Grace nodded.

Allison smiled. "Good luck then." She slid out the door with everyone else.

"Grace?" Stubblefield pointed to the photo. "Is this your father?"

"Uh huh." She cleared her throat. "He dug up the juniper on Sunday, and it . . . he . . . had his stroke the very next day." She stiffened. Why had she said that? That was her own personal business.

Of course, she was pretty sure Stubblefield knew the whole sad story. Grace had been in school when her father had his stroke, and they called her into a guidance counselor's office to wait for Angela, who drove Grace to the hospital. Diana had said that any time you set foot in a guidance counselor's office, for any reason, it went on your permanent record.

Stubblefield laid the photo on his desk and chuckled, which surprised Grace. "This Japanese is a serious interest, I see."

Grace glanced at her hand. The faint outline of the *Zo* was still there. And, of course, the Asian gang story would have been passed around the teacher's lounge. She shook her head. "Not really," she said. "I just like the way the characters look." The words were automatic, as if she were only repeating what someone else had said. Only the someone else was her.

"We don't offer it here," Stubblefield said, "but I could get you into the critical languages program over at the community college."

Grace collected her tools and photo. "No," she said. "It's just something I have fun with."

Stubblefield raked back his hair. "Grace, as a teacher, I can tell you we fall down on our knees in gratitude for any student who still has fun with anything."

Grace looped the straps of her backpack over one shoulder and hooked her arm around the bonsai pot. "Well, as a student," she said, "I don't care."

Stubblefield laughed. She had thought he would.

"I've got to take a math test." She patted the outside pocket of the pack to make sure she had her calculator.

"Well, at least think about it," Stubblefield said as she left the room.

Yeah, Grace thought as she ran down the long hall, I'll put that on my list.

19

Mr. Frankel's classroom was over in the science building, where all the labs were located. Lab space was one thing they'd made a big deal about in the newspaper, when the school was being built, when everyone was upset about being moved. Diana had said it was all just propaganda, that the newspaper was the government's shill. Grace peeked in one open door. The lab was definitely bigger than the one she'd worked in back at Parkwood. Cleaner, with more sinks. People had fought over sinks at Parkwood. Physically.

Grace looked at the number on the door. 1003L. She moved down to the next door—1005—and looked inside. The room was empty, but WILLIAM FRANKEL, MATHEMATICS was posted on the door. She went in and sat down in the middle of the front row. She took out two pencils, her calculator, and two sheets of paper. She looked at her watch. He had said 2:45. Two minutes to spare.

The walls of the room were lined with posters filled with formulas and wild-haired science types. She'd never seen Mr. Frankel, but she'd heard he was old. She picked up the two pieces of paper. Debated them in her head. Put them away.

She'd let him make the call on paper. Teachers loved to give permission.

"Miss Morrison?" The deep voice wrapped around the room.

Grace looked around. Mr. Frankel's hair was white, but there was plenty of it. He wasn't tall, but he stood up sharp and erect. He wore a gray suit that nipped in slightly at the waist. He bore no resemblance to the rumpled men in his posters.

"Yes, sir," she said.

He opened a yellow file folder and studied it as he walked up the aisle. He lifted up a paper, nodded briefly at the one underneath, then closed the folder.

"Okay," he said and sat down at his desk. Grace shifted in her desk and looked at him. She could feel her right foot tapping, but she couldn't stop it. She'd gone through only about half of that stupid math book, and she wasn't sure she remembered much of that. She needed to take the test right now.

"So, Miss Morrison," Mr. Frankel said. "I see that you were one of the students who was transferred over from Parkwood."

Grace nodded.

He looked up.

"Yes, sir," she said.

"The transition, I understand, has been disruptive for many students."

Grace emphatically ceased her foot tapping. " I guess," she said. She pressed her teeth together.

"A few years ago"—he smiled and shook his head—"I

encountered a wonderful young math student in my class. Her name was Elizabeth Hardy."

Grace straightened up. Elizabeth Hardy had been her math teacher last year at Parkwood.

Mr. Frankel nodded, laid down the file, walked around to the front of his desk and hopped up onto it.

Grace smiled. It was odd to see such a proper man hop. It was even odder to see how proper he still looked, with his feet dangling a few inches from the floor.

Mr. Frankel looked down at his hands. "I will admit I argued fervently"—he looked up at Grace—"against her becoming a high school math teacher, but"—he shook his head—"to no avail." He nodded slightly. "I understand she's quite a good one, though."

Grace nodded. "Yes, sir," she said. "Very good."

Mr. Frankel folded his arms over his chest. "Well," he said, "I had a lengthy discussion with Miss Hardy yesterday afternoon, and we both agree that my class would, indeed, be more appropriate for your abilities." He reached behind his back for a text and some papers. He held them up, pushed away from the desk, and put the materials down in front of Grace. "I'll notify Ms. Jackson and Ms. Kennedy."

Grace picked up the new math textbook. It was smaller and less colorful than her other one. She looked at Mr. Frankel. "What about the test?"

He shook his head. "It's not necessary." He was already stuffing his briefcase and straightening his desk, as if he were ready to leave. "I have all the information I need."

Grace stood up.

Mr. Frankel's back was to her. "See you on Monday," he said. "Check the syllabus."

Grace's eyelids fluttered. She couldn't quite catch her breath. "No." She sat down. "I want to take the test." She wasn't going to fall for that again. She wasn't going to let someone pencil her in just so they could turn around and erase her.

Mr. Frankel turned and faced her. "I beg your pardon?" He bent his arm to check his slim gold watch.

"I want to take the test," Grace said. "I don't want you to just let me in the class. I want . . ." Her hand trembled. "I need proof."

Mr. Frankel nodded. "Well"—he stroked his chin—"you've taken me by surprise, Miss Morrison. I must admit that I was too presumptuous to foresee this response." He folded his arms. "As it turns out, I made plans to meet a friend in half an hour."

"Oh." Grace felt suddenly very stupid. "Well." She had what she wanted. "Okay, then." She was out of Kennedy's class.

He held up his hand. "That's none of your concern, of course, but let's see if this plan works for you. We proceed with the necessary paperwork. You show up in my class on Monday. If, by next Friday, you still desire to take this test, I promise to set aside time to administer it to you." He unfolded his arms. "Agreed?"

"Yes, sir." Grace stood up. She bit her lip. "You see, sir, the way it is, one person can say one thing on Friday, and on Monday, somebody else can come at you with something completely different. And Kennedy will—"

"Ms. Kennedy," Mr. Frankel said.

"Ms. Kennedy," Grace said.

"Do you have your old math text?"

Grace nodded. Already, she thought, it was old. "Yes, sir." She pulled it out of her backpack.

Mr. Frankel held out his hand. "I'll return it when I notify Ms. Kennedy."

Grace gave it to him. "Thank you, sir."

Mr. Frankel continued as if she hadn't spoken. "People, Miss Morrison—their characters and abilities and accomplishments—accumulate. Every day is not an absolute beginning. Perhaps not on this particular afternoon, but you have been tested, and you have passed." He paused. "B+." He raised his eyebrows. "Good enough?"

"Yes, sir," Grace said. "Thank you."

He looked at his watch. "Very well," he said.

Grace left the room slowly, but she picked up speed in the hall. Her feet seemed to barely touch the floor. Mr. Frankel had heard her. Seen who she was. He'd actually researched her.

The city bus was only about half full. Grace swayed down the aisle and snuggled into a middle seat. She pulled the cord at Campbellton Road and dragged herself off. She waved to Ed and Johnny and looked up at the sign. MORRISON'S GARAGE AND BODY SHOP. When the shop was sold, Grace had assumed the MORRISON'S would come down. Her mother had laughed when she asked her about it. "Half of what they paid us for that place, they paid us for the name. The reputation."

Just like Mr. Frankel had said, Grace thought. Her father might be in a wheelchair. You could just barely understand his words. But just the same, all that had come before mattered.

Her father was out on the front porch. Sophie was behind him, pulling his arms up and out, which was part of his therapy. No one else had been able to get him out into the fresh air, but in the short time Sophie had been there, Grace had seen them out on the porch at least three times. Patty sent up a screech from the backyard; Mrs. Morrison was probably out with her.

Grace went into her bedroom and closed the door on all of them. She wiggled down into her pillow and folded the comforter over her legs. You had your random events. Your pencils. Erasers. Massive strokes. Your Kennedys and Saylerses. Even your Frankels. But then you also had your accumulation. Your ammunition. Your you.

Grace pulled the spread higher and tighter. She was almost glad the whole homeschooling thing hadn't worked out for her. She sort of liked the idea of taking them on on their own turf.

20

Now that Patty had gotten old enough to really appreciate it, Mrs. Morrison had settled back into her old habit of cooking pancakes and sausage on weekend mornings. Consequently, Grace had given up her habit of sleeping until noon on Saturdays. Maybe, Grace thought, as she stumbled into the kitchen at nine o'clock, that was her mother's intent. To get her out of bed at a *decent* hour.

This morning, though, there were only open boxes of bagels and doughnuts on the table. And instead of puttering over Patty, her mother sat at the table with Sophie.

"Help yourself," Sophie said.

Grace picked out a whole wheat bagel and stuck it in the toaster. "Where's Patty?" she asked.

Brochures and pamphlets and printouts were spread between Sophie and her mother. Mrs. Morrison looked up from the one she was holding. "Didn't you hear about Angela's promotion? She's on straight first, which means weekends off."

"She took Patty out for breakfast." Sophie pushed a brochure to her mother and tapped her finger on it. "Look," she said. "This one meets on Saturdays. That would be good."

Mrs. Morrison adjusted her glasses and studied the blurb. She nodded. She looked up at Sophie. "$425."

"Mom," Sophie said. "That's nothing. Just show it to them. I promise you, they won't blink." She looked up, snapped her fingers, and pointed at the coffee pot on the counter.

Grace, who was leaning beside it, raised her eyebrows.

Sophie nodded. "And if they do, then ask what they recommend."

Grace filled her cup. "Will there be anything else, ma'am?"

Sophie looked up. "That'll be all." She smiled. "For now." She leaned in closer to her mother. "Just do it."

Grace smeared her bagel with some cream cheese and sat down. She pulled one of the brochures closer with her finger. Piedmont Community. She nodded. "Oh," she said. "You know Mr. Stubblefield, my social studies teacher?"

Mrs. Morrison nodded.

"He was just talking to me about Piedmont. He said I could take a class there."

"Right now? While you're in high school?"

Grace nodded. "At least a Japanese class."

Her mother frowned. "Japanese?"

"Oh, yeah." Sophie nodded. "She was writing in Japanese." She tapped the back of her hand.

Mrs. Morrison leaned back and looked at them. She had no comment. Grace laughed. "So?" She asked Sophie. "Are you going to school there?"

Sophie nodded at her mother. "I will if she will."

"Mom?"

"Yes." Sophie passed Grace a dark glance. "Mom." She

patted her mother's hand. "You know how she's been volunteering over at the physical therapy center?"

Grace shook her head. She knew her mother took her father over there twice a week, but she didn't know anything about her mother's volunteering.

"Well"—she squeezed her mother's hand—"they are so impressed with her over there, they offered her a paying job."

"Just part time," Mrs. Morrison interjected.

"Because that's all you agreed to," Sophie said. She touched Grace's hand and nodded. "And they offered to pay for a computer class, to bring her up to speed on their system."

Her mother wrapped her fingers around her cup. "I don't know." She looked through the window over the sink. Grace followed her glance. She saw her father parked in his chair, out in the backyard, by himself. "How did he get out there?" Grace asked.

Sophie reached over and broke off a little piece of one of the doughnuts. "I pushed him out through the garage." She raised herself up a little to look at him. "He needs to be able to do it by himself, though, whenever he wants." She gulped down the last of her orange juice. "Angela said there's this guy she works with who does light construction on the side, and she's been talking to him about building a ramp."

Mrs. Morrison sighed. "But they say he can still make a lot of progress. He might not need a ramp."

"Fine," Sophie said. "But I'm talking about now."

Mrs. Morrison stood up and poured herself a cup of coffee. "That therapy is hard." She took a sip. "It takes a lot of motivation. I don't want him to get too comfortable. I don't want him to get . . . stuck."

Sophie shook her head. "I don't see him getting too comfortable, Mom."

Mrs. Morrison looked out the window and studied her husband. "I'm not sure it does him good to be out there. All he does is sit and stare at the shop."

"And how," Sophie asked, "is that worse than sitting and staring at four walls?"

Grace lifted her cup, pulled back in her chair to take a sip, and watched the conversation escalate into the inevitable jabbing.

Mrs. Morrison shrugged. "You want to make him happy?" she said. "Figure out a way to roll that chair under a car."

"Mom!" Sophie dropped her jaw and just let it hang there a moment. Mrs. Morrison clattered her cup down on the counter. "He's not that far gone. What a horrible thing to say."

Mrs. Morrison blinked. "Oh my . . ." She pressed her palm against her chest. "What I meant, Sophie, is that what would really make your father happy is if he could be back under a car . . . *working on it*." She looked at Grace. "How does she come up with these things?"

Grace laughed. She imagined her father rolling into that dialogue.

"Look at this, Mom." Sophie pinched off another bit of the doughnut. "They have a Physical Therapist Assistant Degree."

Mrs. Morrison shook her head. "I'll be working in the office."

"Oh." Grace nodded. That made sense. Even though Grace had never really thought of her mother as working, she had always kept the books for the shop.

"No," Sophie said. "I meant for me." She turned the page. "Or this," she said. "Veterinary Technology."

Mrs. Morrison smiled and turned back to look at her husband.

Sophie clattered her chair away from the table, stood up, and looked at Grace. "You don't have to work today, right?"

Grace shook her head.

Sophie looked at her mother. "See?"

"Okay, then," Mrs. Morrison said. "If you want, I'll drive you over to take that test for your driver's license." She rinsed her cup and set it in the sink.

Grace didn't say anything.

Her mother nodded. "I know I'm springing this on you."

"No, no." Grace stood up. "Let me get my shoes. I'm ready."

Mrs. Morrison pushed her hair behind her ears. "Okay, then." Grace ran back to her room for her shoes and her wallet. "Go ahead and pull the car out," her mother called after her. "Get the feel of it."

"She drives my car all the time," Sophie said. "She'll do just fine."

Grace bit her lip. Another day, another test, she thought. And this sure wasn't going to be like Frankel's math test. No deputy sheriff was going to slide onto the seat beside her, say, "Sophie said you were just fine," and give her a driver's license. Still, Grace felt confident. At least about regular driving. Parking worried her. The last time she'd parallel parked had been months ago with her dad. While she waited for her mother, Grace tried to manipulate into a pretend space in the driveway, but it didn't work. She needed real barriers—at least a curb—to judge how she was doing.

Sophie ran down the steps ahead of her mother. Grace let down her window, and Sophie leaned in. "You keep on her about that class," she said. "She's too young to just retire."

Grace looked up at her mother hurrying down the front steps. *Young*, she thought. She nodded. From Sophie's point of view, their mother was pretty much the right age.

Mrs. Morrison settled back into the passenger seat. "All right," she said. "Let's go." She folded her arms.

Grace turned to back down the driveway and glanced at her mother. Point of view, whether it was hers or Sophie's or anyone else's, shouldn't matter so much. Her mother should just be who she was, and that should be that. The same way Grace shouldn't walk from Ms. Kaye's class into Kennedy's and feel like two different people.

"I don't know what Sophie's thinking sometimes," Mrs. Morrison said.

"You mean the veterinary science thing?"

Her mother smiled. "Well, yes, but she had some idea that she could bring you out here, that she could pass for your mother."

"Oh, yeah."

"How would that look?" She shook her head. "That girl is so impulsive." She looked at Grace. "It didn't kill you to wait a bit, now did it?"

Grace shrugged. "No, ma'am."

The pavement suddenly appeared darker and wet. The branches of the trees were dripping as if there had been a downpour, but the sun appeared to have broken through for good now. "What about that?" her mother said. "With all that sunshine back at the house." She laughed. "When they said scattered showers, they meant scattered showers."

Grace frowned. The kids at school had told her that the testing center closed for rain. Even a drizzle. She slowed down at the first of several green, official-looking signs; she knew the testing center was around here somewhere. Labor Commission. State Employee Credit Union. The third one said "Driver's License Testing Center." Grace carefully signaled and turned in. She felt as if she were being watched already.

"Everyone's in such a hurry," Mrs. Morrison said.

Grace slowed down even more. She eased on the brake as she looked around for a parking space. Everyone always told her parking here was impossible, but right off she saw three vacant spots.

"But no one's ever been in as big a hurry as Sophie."

Grace bypassed the first one and went for the second, wider space. Her mother wasn't commenting on her driving. She was still on Sophie. Which didn't bother Grace so much today. It was like Sophie had said—*I'm here to take the heat in person now.*

The line was long enough that six people waited outside the door to the building. They were all dripping wet. One of the girls was completely soaked, with dripping hair and running mascara.

A man pointed down to the end of the parking lot. "Thirty minutes ago," he said, "the line snaked all the way down there, but when the storm blew up, they put up the Closed sign and told us to go home."

The line jerked forward, and two people moved through the

door. Mrs. Morrison looked at Grace. "Do you think it's possible that we got lucky?" She looked as if she didn't.

Grace looked up at the sky, then checked out the OPEN sign. "I think maybe," she said.

They really did. Two hours later, Grace had her license and was driving her mother home. And from the horror stories she'd heard at school, she knew that could very well be record time.

"Well, will you look at that?" Mrs. Morrison said when they pulled into the driveway.

Grace looked over and saw her father sitting on the porch. Johnny sat beside him, talking and shuffling a stack of papers. "That's nice of him," she said. "To come over." She pulled up under the tree and cut the engine.

Mrs. Morrison laughed. "Knowing Johnny, he's over here because he needs something." She shook her head. "Not that I mind," she said. "Being needed means a lot more than being nice." As they walked toward the door, she put her hand on Grace's shoulder and said, "Congratulations."

21

As soon as Grace turned into Diana's driveway, she regretted it. It was steep and narrow, with no place to turn around. She recalled how Kate always had to navigate her way down the street in reverse. Grace pulled in between two overgrown bushes and tried not to think about it.

The back door was unlocked. Grace went onto the porch and rapped on the kitchen door. Then she saw Ted. He lifted his head up off the table and pushed his hair out of his face. His hair was like Diana's; it just stayed wherever he put it. He opened his eyes wider, shook his head, and stumbled to his feet.

"Didn't mean to wake you up," Grace said. "I didn't see you."

Ted yawned. "I wasn't asleep." He stepped back, nodded at the chair to his right, and sat down.

Grace sat down. The house was unusually quiet.

"I was thinking." He waved his hand over the papers and forms strewn on the table.

Grace picked up one of the forms. She looked at Ted. "You're going to college in Rhode Island?"

"Doubtful." He picked up the plastic jug of mango juice and took a swig. "You want something to drink?" He thumbed at the refrigerator. "This is really good, but"—he shrugged—"I thought I'd finish it before anyone else showed up." He winked. "Don't tell my mom."

Grace opened the refrigerator and took out a root beer. "Are these applications hard to fill out?"

"Not too bad," he said. "It's the essay questions." He slid one of the forms to her and jabbed at the bottom of the page. "I've got to get this in early, to be considered for a scholarship."

Grace read the question. *What do you consider the single most important event in determining the direction of your life so far?* "That's a tough one," she said. "For me, anyway."

He slid a piece of paper to her. He'd written "First of all," drawn a line through that, then written "Initially." He took another swig of mango juice. "I think I've got a handle on it," he said. "What do you think?"

Grace slid the paper back to him. "You've got a ways to go." She was disappointed. She'd thought she was about to find out something fundamental and new about Ted—*single most important event*—but all she found out was that he was funny. Which she already knew.

"I don't like the way they put it," Ted said. "There's no one big single thing that happened on one particular day." He shrugged. "You've met my Grandpa Henry."

Grace nodded.

"He had this huge influence on my life, but only because of little, everyday things, over a long time." He sighed. "And it took me a long time to know it." He shook his head. "I don't know."

"No." Grace said. "I know —*exactly*—what you mean." She looked over her shoulder. "Diana's not here?"

Ted tapped the eraser end of his pencil on the table. "She ought to be here soon. Mom went to get her." He nodded at the door. "She's over at that art thing."

"Oh, yeah. I forgot."

"She called about an hour ago." He stretched his arms over his head. "All excited." He wiggled his fingers. "Oooo, Mommy, I sold my pot." He took on his shrill Diana voice. "I'm a professional artist."

"I got my license today."

"Driver's?" Ted said. "Fishing? Hunting?"

Grace grinned. "To kill," she said.

He leaned forward. "Want to take me for a ride?"

"I would, but—"

Ted nodded. "But your mother said you could only drive straight here and straight back."

Grace nodded. Except that her mother had said "directly." Directly to Diana's and directly back.

"It'll pass." Ted patted her hand. "So," he said. "How's the party thing going?"

Grace cleared her throat. He brought it up. Another sign. An opportunity. Now or never. "Actually"—Grace took a deep breath—"I need your help."

Ted frowned.

Grace tried to lay it out logically. The way Allison had presented it to her. Number one, Allison would be at her dad's office. Number two, Ted would be making an afternoon delivery to the office.

Ted interrupted her there. "How do you know that?"

133

"You will, right?"

He nodded and resumed frowning. Grace continued trying to explain how easy it would be.

Ted chugged the mango juice. "That's a hell of a thing to ask me to do, Grace." He raked his hair. "I don't even know the girl. Why would she come anywhere with me?"

Grace closed her eyes. "Okay." She put her hands on the table. She opened her eyes. "Let's say you're there. She's there. And it works out."

Ted scrunched up his face. "I don't know."

Grace held up her hand. "Let's just say, if it happens, it happens."

"But, otherwise," Ted said, "it doesn't?"

"Exactly," Grace said. "Otherwise, it doesn't."

"And no hard feelings?"

Grace smiled. "Of course not," she said. "If it doesn't, I'll be over at her house. I'll give you her number, so you can just call me. In any case, just come and . . . " She looked down and cleared her throat. "Bring your friends."

Ted folded his arms, leaned back in his chair, and looked at her. "Okay." He tilted his head a bit. "If it happens."

A warm rush of gratitude washed over Grace. He was right. It was an outrageous request. Grace watched herself stand up, take his face in her hands, and kiss him square on the mouth. Not in a hard, cheesy way, but in a solid, affectionate way. "You are so sweet," she heard herself say. She winced. *Sweet*. That was the problem with words. Too many people had access to them. They were hopelessly tainted.

"So, okay?" Ted blinked at her from across the table.

Grace nodded. "Yeah." She pushed her chair away from the table. "I'll let you get back to your essay."

"I think I'll give it a few days." He pulled the papers together and shuffled them. "Maybe some single most important thing will come up."

"Maybe." Come essay time for her, Grace thought, she wouldn't have anything to write about. Not unless some of the scenes in her head started playing out in the real world.

Diana banged through the back door. "I sold my bowl!" She waved four bills in the air.

Grace jumped up and threw her arms over her head. "I got my driver's license!"

Diana shrieked.

Ted stood up, took his jug and his papers, and left the room.

22

One week and counting. On Monday, Hannah called a meeting of the party committee. She rolled a pencil between her fingers. "First of all—"

Grace dropped her head and smiled. "First of all" reminded her of Ted's essay. He really hadn't put up much of a fight at all. And if it hadn't been for Allison's crazy idea, Grace wouldn't even have necessarily thought to invite him.

"—should be easy," Hannah concluded.

"Easy?" Grace asked.

Hannah frowned. "Food," she said. "Food should be easy."

"What about a cake?" Diana asked.

"Well, if you want to make one," Hannah said, "we can do a big sheet cake from a mix, and you guys can decorate it however you like."

Diana nodded. "I like the white pudding kind." She looked at Grace. "With fudge frosting."

Hannah screwed up her nose. "Could we go the other way? White on chocolate? It's much more festive."

Diana shrugged. Grace nodded.

"Or"—Hannah laid her pencil on her desk—"Sue said she would order one to be delivered to the house before the party."

Grace raised her hand. "That gets my vote." Sounded easy. Grace saw herself opening up the Andersons' big front door and taking a box from a delivery guy.

Diana hesitated. "It would be fun, though, to decorate the cake."

Hannah flipped up her hand. "I vote for delivery." She tilted her head at Diana. "Don't worry. Some signature opportunities will arise."

Grace didn't know what Hannah meant by that, but Diana smiled and leaned back. Apparently she did. Hannah turned her arm and checked her watch. She'd gone monochrome again today, but this time in rich brown. Her shirt was a simple little V-neck shell, but it rode her every movement perfectly. Like liquid. Grace wondered if she could find one like it in black.

"Between me and Tara, I guess we've lined up about forty people."

Hannah tapped her pencil. "So"—she looked past them and pressed her lips together—"between the no-shows and the tagalongs, let's say"—she wrote something on her pad and circled it—"forty." She looked up. "I'm bringing along Sidney for quality control."

Grace and Diana looked at each other. Diana had told Grace she'd overheard some sort of argument between Sidney and Hannah on Saturday. Grace was glad they'd made up; Sidney was deadly handsome, and she could tell Hannah really liked him.

Hannah lifted her pencil and twirled it. "What about the guest of honor?"

Grace blurted out the Ted thing. Diana shook her head. "I can't believe you got him to agree to that," she said.

Hannah looked puzzled. "That sounds a little . . . convoluted to me." She leaned back. "Wouldn't it be easier for one of you—"

"But," Grace said, "Ted would be better. More out of the blue." She was surprised at how attached she was to the idea that Ted would be there. That was one thing that fascinated Grace about Allison, the way her wacky ideas found their way into the real world.

Hannah shook her head. "If it works."

"That's just it," Grace said. "If it doesn't, Ted said he'll call, so we can run over there and get her. Do something else."

"Which is what we'll probably end up doing," Diana said.

"Okay, then." Hannah dropped her pencil. "Dismissed."

The girls stood up. "Hannah," Grace asked, "where did you get that shirt?"

Hannah tugged at it. "You like it?"

Grace nodded. "I love it."

"At Jean Baptiste," Hannah said. "At the Prado."

On Tuesday, after school, Sophie and Grace drove over to Jean Baptiste. They did have it in other colors. Grace bought a black one, and Sophie picked up a red one.

On Wednesday, Grace found the card from Sue lying on her bed along with the usual junk mail. The card's border was mottled and rough textured, like the envelope, with an old-fashioned, brown-tinted photograph of dried flowers centered on the front. Grace opened and read:

Dear Grace,

Thank you again, so very much, for the consideration and kindness you and Diana have shown Allison. Perhaps it's my imagination, but I sense a bit more contentment in her these past days—and that, of course, I attribute more to friendship than to any single event like a party.

And, of course, you know that my concern and gratitude is also based on selfishness. At first, I was afraid she wouldn't forgive me for bringing her home. So, if you need anything else for the party, do not hesitate to call.

Thanks again!

Sue Anderson

Grace fell back on her pillow and pressed the card against her chest. *Bringing her home.* No, she thought, she certainly didn't know. Allison had told Grace and Diana about sleeping through history, drawing instead of writing a term paper, a screwy shoplifting episode, and the boy in her room, and, even though Grace wasn't sure she'd ever said so outright, Allison had certainly led them to believe she'd been kicked out of Winston. If that were the case, though, why would Sue need Allison to forgive her?

Grace rolled over and pulled the comforter along with her. She closed her eyes. Allison's phone call woke her up just before dinner. They talked about Stubblefield for a while, then went back and forth about the party in the sort of coy code they'd adopted. If it weren't for the Ted thing, Grace thought that by now she would have forgotten herself that this wasn't a for-real surprise party. In her head, it sort of was.

"I had to stay late today, to rehearse that scene with Tara," Allison said.

Grace fingered the edges of Sue's card. "How'd it go?" she asked.

"Not bad," Allison said. "She was totally in character. Not flaky at all. I guess she's pretty good."

Something about Sue's card made Grace sad—the dried flowers as much as the words—so she couldn't bring it up directly. She didn't want to hear Allison laugh about it. "Why is it exactly," Grace asked, "that you didn't go back to Winston?"

Allison hesitated. "You know what's funny?" she said. "Getting into that school was such a big deal that I thought I was a total loser if I didn't go back." Her voice went a little lower. "But somehow I'm a much bigger deal here because I was there, at some time in the past, than I ever was there for actually being there." She laughed. "Does that make any sense?"

"Some," Grace said. The words certainly didn't answer her question, but their tone fit right in with Sue's sad and beautiful card.

After dinner on Thursday, Grace went back into her room, and wiggled into her newest pair of black jeans and her Hannah shirt. She opened her closet, pulled out Sophie's kimono, and slid it on. She took a deep breath and looked in the mirror. Not bad, she thought. Not as serious as Hannah. Not as flashy as Allison. Not as slutty as Sophie. More exotic than Diana. She stepped up on her bed to get a longer view.

She stepped down and was about to change when Sophie blasted through the door. "You want pie or—" Sophie's face filled up with an open-mouthed smile. "You're going to wear it?" She stepped back and nodded. "It looks great, except"— she moved closer and twisted Grace's hair in back—"you ought to wear your hair up."

Grace craned her neck around and looked. Sophie was right. And it would be easy enough. Just twist it up and clip it.

Sophie let go and nodded. "I'm really glad you can use it."

Grace didn't think. She just said it. "I'm really glad you came back."

Sophie laughed. "I'll check with you on that in a week," she said. "I won't hold you to anything." She raised her eyebrows. "Pie?"

* * *

On Friday, Mr. Frankel returned the first quiz Grace had taken in his class. When he gave Grace hers, he said, "For your dossier, Miss Morrison."

She looked down and read: *This work is more than satisfactory for a student in my class. William Henry Frankel.* She blushed.

"I feel certain," he said, "that it will stand up in a court of law." And he moved on up the aisle.

The next day was Allison's birthday party.

23

Grace looked around the kitchen. Another Saturday without pancakes. Her mother sat at the table alone, eating a piece of toast and drinking a cup of coffee.

Grace opened the refrigerator, took out the juice, and poured herself a glassful. "Where is everybody?"

"Well," her mother said, "Angela was taking Patty out to that amusement park, and, all of a sudden, Sophie up and decided she wanted to go, too." Mrs. Morrison shook her head. "You know how Sophie is about those rides. Like a little kid." She hooked her thumb toward the window. "And your dad's out back."

Grace looked through the window. Johnny had pulled one of the plastic chairs beside her father and was leaning in, shuffling papers and talking a mile a minute.

"I guess Sophie was right," Mrs. Morrison said. "Johnny's been having trouble with some vendors and suppliers, and he said he never would have knocked on the door and bothered your father, but when he saw him sitting out back the other day, he just had to come over."

Grace nodded. "Daddy doesn't look as if he minds." Johnny

was drinking a Coke. She remembered how her father used to laugh about how Johnny went through ten or fifteen Cokes a day. "That boy must have an iron stomach," he'd always say.

"Oh, heavens, no," her mother said. "He's giving the boy the lowdown on who you can believe, and who you'd best not turn your back on." Her mother set the empty mug on her saucer and swept a few stray crumbs from the table into her hand. "Which, as we all know, is his favorite topic."

Grace sat down. "Is there anybody Daddy thinks you can believe?"

"Some more than others, I reckon." She stood up and rinsed her dishes in the sink. She smiled at her husband and Johnny.

"Sophie was supposed to take me over to Allison's today. To set up for the party."

Her mother shook her head. "Just take the car," she said.

"You sure?" Grace said. "I'll be gone until tonight." Mostly her mother had restricted her to short, *directly there* and *directly back* trips.

"I'm sure," Mrs. Morrison said.

Diana had some pots to trim and some others to go into the kiln, so she had to go to the Art Center this morning. Hannah said she'd be there finishing up some paperwork, so they could both drive over to Allison's around four-thirty. Sue had arranged for the cake to be delivered at three, though, so Grace had volunteered to go over earlier. Perfect, she had thought. A couple of hours alone in the house.

Even though no one was at home, Grace knocked before she twisted the long, old-fashioned key in the lock. She paused another beat before she turned the regular-looking key in the deadbolt.

Grace stepped into the kitchen and stood still for a moment. She missed the sound of the radio in the kitchen, which had always been on, and, always, as far as she could tell, set on NPR. The beeps and clatters, which always emanated from Sue and Dennis, seemed more noticeable now that they were gone.

She laid her party clothes over the back of a chair and wandered through the dining room. Into the sunroom. Down the hallway and to the green room. She stood on the orange-and-green carpet and stretched out her arms. She sat on the edge of the daybed just for a minute, then went back through the den to the front room with the big window. Allison had said that was where they put up their Christmas tree.

She opened the cover on the black baby grand piano. Allison said she could play Bach, but she wouldn't. She said that she'd been forced to take lessons for twelve years, that she had hated every minute of it, and that she wasn't about to give Sue and Dennis the satisfaction of hearing her actually play. Grace's finger hovered over the keys, but she couldn't bring herself to rip into the silence.

Through the French doors. Back into the kitchen. Grace retrieved her clothes and ran up the stairs to Allison's room. She hung her clothes on the closet door. Curled against a pillow in the window seat. Pulled the plaid blanket and the quiet beauty of the whole place and time up over her. Looked out at the branches loaded with yellow and red leaves. Watched the odd one float down to the street. Just as she had imagined.

It was almost three-thirty when the cake man finally drove

up in a silver van. Grace watched him pull a huge box out of the back and galloped down the stairs to open the door and help him maneuver it into the dining room.

"You need to check it before you sign off," he said. "See if it's right."

Grace loosened the tabs and lifted the top of the box. "It's beautiful," she said. The background was mostly a light pink, with big red roses clustered in the corners, with lots of little roses running all over it like vines, with, of course, *Happy Birthday, Allison!* Grace reached down and touched one of the big roses. It was real. Grace sighed.

"Well?" The guy pushed his clipboard at her. Grace signed, walked him to the front door, and watched him climb back into his van. It struck her that she'd only noticed the words on the cake, not actually examined them. She ran back to the dining room and lifted the top of the box. They might have spelled *Allison* with one *l* or even a *y*, but they hadn't. It was beautiful and decorated, she was sure, just the way Sue wanted, but Grace still couldn't say it was exactly right. Not perfect. Not for *Allison*.

She walked to the door of the sunroom and looked out through the long row of windows. What kind of cake would be exactly right for Allison, she wondered. Midnight blue with glittery silver stars and a moon, maybe. It wouldn't be the whole truth, but it would be closer than roses.

The telephone rang. Ted sprang to her brain. Despite his ambivalent promise, and despite the number of times she'd explained the logic of the plan to other people, Grace still couldn't bring the picture of Ted and Allison in Allison's dad's office, getting into his car, driving here—any of it—into focus. She picked up in the kitchen. "Hello?"

"It's a disaster." Diana.

Grace squeezed the receiver. "What?"

"Kevin let the temperature go too high," she said. "Everything in the kiln blew up."

Grace looked through the door at the cake on the dining table. She had an odd flash of it flying into a kaleidoscope of red petals and pink frosting pieces.

"For heaven's sake." Hannah. "It's not a disaster. I'll be over shortly. Diana's staying to help clean up and reload the kiln. Sandra lives over that way and will drop Diana off later."

"Okay." Grace wasn't quite sure what to say. "I'm sorry."

"These things happen," Hannah said.

"Let me talk to Diana."

"Hey," Diana said.

"Did you lose anything?"

"No," Diana said, "but it's a disaster."

"Allison's cake came," Grace said. "It's huge. It has real flowers on it."

"Wow," Diana said. "What kind?"

"Roses."

Hannah came back on. "Shortly," she said.

Grace hung up and walked upstairs. She snuggled back into Allison's window seat and closed her eyes. Her images of the party receded, almost as if they were memories of something that had already happened. Grace closed her eyes.

24

People gathered in the front yard. Sue and Dennis beat on the door with their fists. Allison yelled up angry words that Grace couldn't understand. She watched them for a few minutes before floating down the stairs and settling into a high-backed leather chair. All the doors were locked. Grace curled up her legs and listened.

She jerked to attention. The banging was loud and insistent. She kicked off the cover, jumped out of the window seat, and galloped down the stairs.

"Grace!" Hannah yelled.

"I'm coming!" Grace yelled back. She ran through the kitchen and opened the back door.

"What were you up to?" Hannah shifted a paper grocery bag at Grace.

"You won't believe it." Grace laughed. "I fell asleep."

Hannah set the other bag on the counter. "Brilliant," she said. "Now me, I'd be playing dress-up in Sue's closet." She looked up and down and around. Grace could see that the oversized bowls in the space between the ceiling and the cabinets interested her. "Sleeping in her bed is very subtle." She nodded at Grace. "Much more subversive."

"I was in the window seat," Grace said. "Up in Allison's bedroom."

"Ah," Hannah said. "More romantic then."

"Is everything all right?" Grace asked. "With the kiln and all?"

"Oh," Hannah said. "It was a disaster." She moved to the door and looked into the dining room. "I talked to Sue"—she looked left and right—"and she thought this area—den, dining room, sunroom—ought to be our primary space." She shuffled her feet on the hardwood floor. "Oooh," she said. "Excellent dance floor."

"Hannah," Grace said. "It's not that kind of party."

"Oh?" Hannah asked. "What kind of party is it? Bunch of losers sitting around eating pizza?" She shook her head. "I don't think so." She laughed. "Believe me," she said. "People dance." She walked across the room. "Sue said something about a music system."

"It's in a cabinet in the den, but it's hooked up"—Grace pointed up—"to speakers up there, and maybe—" She walked over to the sunroom and looked in. "Yeah, looks like two out here."

"Sounds simple enough," Hannah said. "Go see if you can actually get it to work." She lifted a chair away from the table and moved it to the wall. "I'll get started out here."

Grace had seen Allison switch on the system a couple of times in what appeared to be a simple single motion. She inserted a CD. It played, but the sound was muffled. She peeked into the dining room. Nothing at all seemed to be coming out of those speakers.

"Here." Hannah wrapped her fingers around one edge of the dining table. "Help me move this over just a bit."

"Okay." Grace frowned.

"We can do it," Hannah said. "I just want to nudge it over a little."

Grace shrugged and lifted her end off the floor. They shifted the table maybe a couple of inches to the left, but that seemed to satisfy Hannah. She swung her arm back and forth. "Lots of traffic through here," she said.

"Oh." Grace smiled. "Traffic patterns."

"Exactly." Hannah smiled back.

Hannah opened up the cake box. "Oh, my." She couldn't stop herself either; she reached in and touched one of the roses. She looked at Grace. "Exquisite." She closed the box. "Predictable, impractical, but exquisite."

Grace looked at the dining table. "My mother was always moving furniture around when she was at home alone, and my father would just have a fit."

Hannah lifted another chair and scanned the opposite wall. "Why?" She moved the chair to the opposite end of the table and set it down. "Why did he have a fit?"

"Because the stuff was too big and heavy for her to move around by herself. She might have hurt herself." Grace moved the chair on her end to the wall. "We couldn't even figure out how she did it."

"I'm sure she had her reasons," Hannah said.

"She said she didn't want to listen to everyone's opinion."

Hannah nodded. "Which was what?" she asked. "That everything was just fine where it was?"

"Yeah." Grace laughed. "I guess."

Hannah stopped fussing around and looked at Grace. "How's your mother these days?"

"They offered her some kind of job at my dad's physical therapy place, and she's talking about taking a computer course at the community college." Grace shrugged. "Okay, I guess."

Hannah knelt down and opened up the lower doors of the buffet. "Maybe you can cut a deal." She closed the doors, straightened up, and caught herself in the mirror on the wall. She dropped her left eyelid and rubbed at the corner. "Your mother can go to school, and you can stay home."

Grace shrugged. "I don't care so much about that anymore." She went back into the den and examined the buttons. One cluster referred to SPKRs. She pressed the first one. Nothing. Then the next one. The dining room speakers blasted. Grace scrambled for volume control. She peeked out into the dining room and said, "Sorry!" but Hannah was in the kitchen.

Grace went through every one of the SPKR buttons before she gave up on the sunroom speakers. Hannah had shimmied up onto the kitchen counter and managed to bring down one of the big bowls. She turned the inside of the bowl toward Grace. "Think it's worth cleaning?" A dusty, oily layer of filth covered the surface. "For chips?"

Grace stuck out her tongue. "No." She opened one of the lower cabinets. "There are some good bowls under here." She reached all the way to the back and pulled out a bright flowery one; it was the same pattern as the Tahiti mug.

"Yeah, okay." Hannah hopped down, rummaged around and came out with a few other receptacles. They filled bowls with chips and dip and a big plate with baby carrots. Grace was out setting some of them in the sunroom when the phone rang.

Grace ran back inside. Ted, she thought. Finally. Hannah held up her finger. She let the answering machine kick in.

"It's Diana."

Grace grabbed the receiver. "Do you have your car or—?"

"Yeah," Grace said. "You need me to come get you?"

"No." Diana took a deep breath. "Sandra lives just down the street from Allison, so she can bring me, but she's got to take her son to a soccer game or something, so she doesn't have time to run me by to get my clothes. I should have brought them with me, but—"

"What?" Hannah asked.

"And I'm a total mess," Diana said.

Grace looked at Hannah. "She needs me to go get her clothes."

Hannah nodded. "You can pick up some ice while you're out."

"You won't believe what I did," Diana said.

Hannah held up a couple of paper lanterns and nodded at the door.

Grace looked at her watch. "Hannah needs me," she said. "Is the key still under the rock?"

"Yeah," Diana said. "My khakis—the ankle cuts—are on the dryer. I got a new shirt—it's blue—and it's hanging on my closet door."

Grace watched Hannah climb up a railing outside. "Okay," she said. "No problem. I've got to go. See you."

151

25

Grace slowed down to turn into Diana's driveway but thought better of it. She didn't want to get stuck in that maze again. She rolled back and parked under the maple tree. She pulled up the flat stone beside the back steps and found the key.

She saw the khakis right away, folded on the dryer on the porch. She checked the label, just to be sure they were the ankle cuts, and went into the kitchen. Instead of following her usual route to Diana's bedroom, she detoured through the back hallway.

She pushed open the door at the end of the hall and hesitated. She hadn't been in Ted's room in years. When they were kids, she had wandered in and out of there, the same as every other room in the Henry house. She sat down on Ted's rumpled bed. Probably around seventh grade, she thought, was the last time she'd been in there. Ted moved on once he was in high school; he didn't pay much attention to them and vice versa. Grace remembered the doors to the back hallway and to Ted's room always being open when she was little. Then, suddenly, they were always closed.

The collection of little gold-colored trophies was still stashed on the shelf in the corner. As far as she knew, Ted hadn't played on any sort of team since junior varsity basketball in ninth grade, and all these trophies were from when he was a kid.

The first time Grace had seen the display, she had stopped to gawk. "How'd you get all those?"

Ted, who had been stretched out on his bed with his eyes closed, said, "I showed up." He didn't open his eyes. "Most of the time."

"They're self-esteem trophies," Diana had explained.

Grace snaked through the jumble of shoes and books on his floor. Passed through the big bathroom into Diana's bedroom. The blue shirt hung on the doorknob. She slipped the pants on the hanger under the shirt, slung them over her left shoulder, and hurried back to the kitchen the way she'd come. She paused before stepping out onto the porch to pinch off a couple of grapes from one of Diana's bowls on the counter. She looked at the clock. Five-thirty. Twenty minutes ago it had seemed as if she had all the time in the world, but now the party pressed hard and fast against her.

The rattle of keys stopped her. The creak of the front door froze her. Kate was in Greenville. Probably Diana's dad, Grace thought. She really didn't have time to get tangled up with him, so she decided to just slip out without saying anything.

Laughter cut through the quiet house. Allison. Grace glanced at the bar that separated the kitchen from the den. Usually the shutters were open, but today, fortunately, the left side was closed. Grace moved back into the kitchen, slipped behind it, and squinted through the slats.

She couldn't see Ted, but she heard him. Stuttering about some *thing* that he had to do for his mother. Apologizing. Promising that he *wouldn't be long.*

What, Grace silently screamed at him, are you doing here? Allison, framed by the door, was fully visible. Her arms were folded under her breasts, then she stretched out her right arm. Her silver bangles clattered. Grace glimpsed fire red nails, which struck her as an ordinary color for Allison.

"Can I help?" Allison asked. "With the *thing?*" Her mouth twisted into a smile. She took on the same tone she had used on Dennis. It wasn't quite as funny, hearing her use it on Ted.

Whatever Ted was doing, he continued rambling on about something.

"Do you," Allison asked, "do this *thing* for your *mother* often?"

Grace took a slow, careful step back, toward the porch.

"Oh, this is just too pathetic." Allison shifted forward. "I know what you're doing. You're killing time until the party."

Grace bit her lip and leaned back in to watch. She heard Ted splutter. He sounded stupid. Grace was glad she couldn't see his face. Then he laughed, and she wished she could.

"Great," he said in the usual slow-and-easy Ted tone.

"The party was my idea to begin with." Allison tilted her head. "No big deal."

Now Grace really wished she could see his face. She strained to hear his muttered response. For the first time she saw Ted; Allison's arm was tangled up around his head. They kissed. Or, at least, it was clear they were coming together one way or another. Grace turned and flew out the back door. She bent her knees, hunched down, and scurried over and across the Bentleys' yard to the car.

She drove like a robot. Programmed for destination. No emotion. No thought. Red means stop. Green means go. Left on Oak. Right on Milton. Right onto Boulevard. Allison's house. Only when she turned off the ignition did her brain kick in. *No big deal.*

Sidney and Tara and some guy with spiky blue hair loped down the steps. "Got the ice?" Sidney asked.

Grace blinked. Ice. Right. She'd—thank goodness—gone to the store first. She popped the trunk. Sidney lifted out one chest, and the blue-haired guy got the other one. Tara closed the trunk. Grace leaned over to the passenger side for the bag with the plastic forks and plates Hannah had also requested. Those words on the side mirror caught her eye.

Tara hovered outside the car door. "I'll take that," she said.

Grace thrust the bag through the window. She looked at the mirror again. *Objects in mirror are closer than they appear.* She thought about the kiss. Not Allison's and Ted's, but the one Grace had trapped in her head last Saturday. The one Ted knew nothing about. She pulled Diana's clothes out of the car and ran up the steps into the kitchen. "Is Diana here?" she asked.

"Upstairs showering." Hannah touched Grace's arm. "One question," she said.

Sidney sidled up between them and nodded toward the dining room. "Kid in there wants to know if you want him to do anything."

Grace looked around. The blue-haired guy was at the sink. "Who?" she asked.

"Very pale, highly ironic young man," Hannah whispered.

Two or three suspects ran through Grace's brain.

Sidney ducked his head down between them. "He's a little heavy on the eyeliner," he whispered.

"Oh," Grace said. "Eric." She twisted toward the hallway. "I need to take these up to Diana."

Hannah held up her finger. "One thing," she said.

Grace nodded. "I'll be right back." Talk about accumulation, she thought.

26

The shower hammered in Allison's bathroom. Grace rattled the knob. Locked. "Diana!" she yelled. "I got your clothes!"

"Great!" Diana yelled back. "Thanks!"

Grace opened her mouth to yell back. Something like "The party's a fake" or "Allison knows," but none of the words seemed to quite get to the point she wanted to make. "I'm sorry" might work, but only for Grace. Diana wouldn't know what she meant.

The doorbell rang. The party. The people. For real, Grace thought. She slipped the black T-shirt over her head and shimmied into her jeans. She sat on the edge of the window seat, for what she felt was the last time, and pulled the brush slowly and deeply through her hair, one section at a time. *Accumulation.* Mr. Frankel's words comforted her. *Every day is not an absolute beginning.* But then, she thought, he hadn't said anything about endings. Could one day be an absolute ending?

The doorbell rang again. Grace stood up, twisted her hair like Sophie had done, and clamped it in place. She slid the kimono off the hanger and over her arms and studied herself in the long mirror on Allison's bathroom door. The little trees circling the hem of the kimono reminded her of the real bonsai in her own bedroom at home. They reminded her of her father before he had his stroke. He had held out the juniper to her and said, "Just throw this in the woods," but she hadn't. She'd seen immediately that it belonged with Cheryl the Potter's pot.

The doorbell rang again. Grace felt the urge to speak to her reflection, to muster some encouraging words to push her downstairs, but even talking to herself she came up empty. For the first time, she truly wished she could speak Japanese. At least form a complete sentence.

The shower stopped. Grace remembered that Hannah had wanted to talk to her about something. She moved to the bathroom door. "Diana?"

"Yeah?"

"Allison knows about the party."

"Probably." Diana laughed. "They always do. On TV anyway."

Grace hesitated. "Your clothes are on the bed," she said and left the room.

A thick red velvet rope was strung across the staircase at the bottom of the stairs. Grace ducked under it and read the sign hanging from the middle of it. NO ADMITTANCE. Like the one blocking off the balcony in the old theater downtown. Grace had to smile. Hannah. She always left her mark. This, she realized, would be considered a signature opportunity.

Hannah glanced out into the hall. "Should we gather everyone in the sunroom?" she asked.

Grace frowned. "Why?"

"For the whole surprise thing," Hannah said. Sidney pushed up behind her and winked at Grace.

Grace felt her face flush. "No." She shook her head. "I think everybody ought to just stand around, doing whatever they're doing." She smiled. She could see it. "It would be funny if no one even said anything to Allison."

"Funny?" Hannah asked.

Tara was hanging off to the side and listening. "Yeah." She nodded.

"I don't mean ignore her," Grace said. "Just don't single her out. Like she's just walked in on a party going on in her own house." Just to mess with her, Grace thought.

Hannah shook her head. "I don't get it."

Sidney slid his arm around Hannah's shoulders. "Sweetheart," he said. "You don't have to get every little thing." He looked at Grace. "Even funnier," he said, "would be—what's the guy's name? That's bringing her?"

"Ted," Grace said.

Sidney nodded. "A couple of kids ought to actually yell out to him, 'Hey, Ted,' or whatever."

"That's great," Tara said. She moved back into the dining room and huddled with some guys.

Grace watched her. Maybe Tara didn't worship Allison as much as she thought.

Hannah sighed. "Yes, but . . ." She looked up at Sidney.

The discussion seemed to shift to one between those two, so Grace drifted into the dining room. Tommy Mullinax, the long-limbed, redheaded basketball player, ducked through the door.

Tommy Mullinax? Grace asked herself, but Tara and, suddenly, Diana were there to answer her.

"He heard me talking to some people about the party," Tara said, "and he said he wanted to come."

"Apparently," Diana said, "he thinks Allison is interesting."

"Interesting as in *odd*," Grace asked, "or as interested *in?*" She didn't see it. Tommy was a jock. Allison was Allison.

"Tara told me what he said," Diana said, "so I called him up. Told him I was Ted Henry's little sister"—she stuck out her tongue—"and he said he'd be here"—she laughed—"and there he is."

Tara cornered another cluster of kids. Grace didn't know her that well, but Tara seemed different today. More animated.

"Weird," Grace said.

Diana gripped her arm. "That's not weird," she whispered. "Here's what's weird. I invited James Albee."

Grace frowned. "The computer guy?" She patted the top of her head. "With the big hair?"

"No," Diana said. "That's James Gilbert. James Albee. The coffee shop guy."

Grace blinked. "With the ponytail?"

"Girls?" They both turned to see Hannah in the kitchen door holding up some pizza boxes.

"I'll get them," Diana said. "He probably just said he'd come to get rid of me." She fingered the sleeve of Grace's kimono. "He's not here."

"It's early," Grace said. She watched Diana take the pizza boxes from Hannah. Watched Tara look up at Tommy Mullinax. Saw Eric give the blue-haired boy a slow punch to the shoulder. Everyone seemed to move at a slightly different speed than usual. The sound of their words didn't quite match up with their mouths.

A key turned in the front door. Grace dropped back. Everyone froze, but just for a second before they remembered the joke and started talking and moving around.

And just for a second, Grace thought, Allison looked annoyed, but her face pulled up so quickly into a big smile that she couldn't be sure.

"Yo, Ted!" some guy yelled out.

"What's up, man?" echoed another. Tara had clearly spread the word.

Allison was into the scene in an instant. She turned to Ted, opened and lifted her arms, and screamed, "Surprise!"

Ted laughed. Allison laughed. Everyone laughed. Perfect, Grace thought. An *icebreaker*. Smooth sailing. No turning back. The party was a success. Everyone would talk about that one moment tomorrow. And they would tell it so much better than it really had been.

27

Grace strolled along the stone path, opened the gate, and ran up the back steps. Hannah didn't look a bit surprised to see Grace come through the kitchen door. As if hiding in the kitchen was exactly where Hannah expected her to be. Grace opened one of the pizza boxes on the counter and lifted out a slice.

With his foot, Sidney pushed a chair away from the table and nodded at Grace. She sat down. Sidney touched her sleeve. "Great kimono," he said. "Very authentic."

Again, Grace knew the perfect response would be an authentic string of Japanese words. All she could say instead was, "It's my sister's."

"Well, to get back to my story," Hannah said. "I don't think I visited Annie . . . " She looked at Sidney. "That was my roommate. In college." She looked at Grace. "Annie."

Grace nodded.

"Right," Sidney said.

"I don't think I visited her more than twice"—she cocked her head—"three times"—she nodded—"three times after we graduated. But, anyway, it was during one of those visits that Dennis called Annie—"

Sidney stood up and knocked on the window. He shook his head and motioned toward the house with his hand. "Couple of guys trampling around back there." He sat down. "Experience tells me," he said, "that the people who live here are very particular about their shrubbery."

"Well," Hannah said, "getting back to my story about those people."

"Sorry," Sidney said.

Hannah shrugged. "Not a story, really, so much as an odd coincidence." She folded her arms across her chest and leaned back. "During one of those very rare visits, Annie got a phone call from Dennis telling her that Sue was pregnant, and so, of course, I got on the phone to congratulate him and all that."

"Huh," Sidney said.

"Otherwise," Hannah said, "I would never even have known they had a daughter or—" She unfolded her arms. "The odd thing is, I was there then." She leaned forward. "And I'm here today." She looked at Grace. "Birthday to birthday. One weird cycle."

Sidney scratched his head. "Well," he said. "It wasn't exactly *birthday* to birthday. This—" he hesitated—"Dennis?"

Hannah nodded. "Dennis," she said. "Sue and Dennis." She held out her arms. "This is their home."

"This Dennis called to say that Sue was pregnant, not that Allison had been born, so—"

"Oh, for heaven's sake," Hannah said. "Close enough."

"Pregnant?" Grace said. "Sue?"

"Yeah," Hannah said. "Dennis called Annie to tell her Sue was pregnant, and I happened to be there."

"Pregnant with who?" Grace asked.

Hannah frowned. "Allison." She pointed toward the dining room. "The birthday girl."

"Allison is adopted," Grace said.

"Where on earth," Hannah asked, "did you get that idea?" She looked at Grace the way her mother did when Grace was sick in bed with a fever. Like she knew Grace was bad off, but she was trying to determine by just how much.

Grace opened her mouth to spill out Allison's story, but, slow as it was, her brain caught up in time to stop it. "Just joking." She stood up and slipped into the hallway. Ducked under Hannah's velvet rope and ran up the stairs. She closed Allison's bedroom door behind her and curled back into the window seat.

Down on the front lawn two guys walked to the front door, punching each other on the arm all the way. Ted's friends, Mark and David. Another figure strolled a few steps behind them. Grace squinted. Bryan Dunne. She could not believe he had come. Allison had been right.

A beat-up little silver car slowed almost to a stop in front of the house, then cruised on past. A couple of seconds later, it came back from the other direction. The car stopped and adjusted. A little forward. A little back. Stop. The door swung open, and a long guy with a ponytail unfolded into the street. Grace pressed her face against the window. James Albee. Coffee Boy.

The noise of the party beat up through the floor. Grace settled back into her corner and pulled the blanket over her

164

knees. Grace closed her eyes. It wasn't as if, in a thousand different ways, Allison didn't let you know what she was doing. Who did she pick as the parent who was not a blood relation? Sue. Sue, with the same blond hair, flamboyant gestures, and dramatic way of talking as Allison.

Grace saw Allison downstairs in the kitchen, fluttering her fingers over her jewels. Heard her saying, "Maybe I'll get the ring made up and just pretend."

She played back Diana's question. "Do you think," Diana had asked, "that everything Allison says is exactly . . . true?"

If Diana had asked Allison that question, she would have said, "Of course not," just as easily as she'd told Ted "no big deal." Grace was the liar. She had kept up a small and petty pretense with her best and oldest friend in the world. And Diana might really and truly not forgive her for that.

Someone tapped at the door and pushed it open. Grace shot up.

"Grace?"

Light poured in behind the figure, and Grace realized she was sitting in total darkness. She reached over, turned on the lamp, and blinked a couple of times to adjust to the light. "What's wrong?"

Ted shook his head. "Nothing." He walked over, pulled the rocker around to face the window seat, and sat down. "What are you doing up here?"

Grace kicked off the blanket and swung her legs around to face him. "Nothing."

"What's that coffee shop guy doing here?" Ted asked. "What's his name?"

"James," she said. "James Albee. Diana invited him."

"Huh." He nodded. "They were dancing."

Grace laughed. "I wish I'd seen that."

"I know. Diana dancing. At a party." He laughed. "At a birthday party."

"Who's dancing with Allison?"

"I don't know." Ted shrugged. "It was easy at first, Grace," he said. "Too easy." He cleared his throat. "She asked *me* for a ride, saying something about not wanting to wait around for her dad, so I didn't have to do anything but say okay." His mouth twisted slightly. "You know that routine."

Grace nodded.

"But then she rushed me out of there so fast, I didn't know what to do with her. We would have gotten here way too early, so I told her I had to drop by my house on the way—"

"I know," Grace said.

Ted straightened up. "I've always thought that girl was a nut," he said. "Now I'm sure."

Grace locked her eyes with his. "Really?"

Ted leaned in. "You know, don't you?" He laughed. "I mean, you know"—he jabbed at his chest—"that I know."

Grace nodded.

"In a weird way, I'm sort of flattered that you used me in your little scheme, but"—he rubbed his chin with his finger—"does Diana know?"

Grace shook her head. "Do you think she'll forgive me?"

"Eventually, I guess." The words screwed slowly out of his mouth. "You know how she is."

Grace saw the kiss again—he was very close—Ted was clear, but the rest of the image blurred into part Allison, part

Grace. She looked out the window and down on the front lawn. Two guys tossed a Frisbee back and forth. She couldn't quite make out who they were. One stumbled over the hem of his trench coat. A drama kid, for sure. She looked back at Ted and stood up. "Well, I guess I'll find out."

Ted pushed up out of the rocker. Grace held up her hand. "Hannah will freak if we go down together." She laughed. "Didn't you see the rope?"

He touched the sleeve of her kimono. "What's this?"

"A Japanese kimono," Grace said. "You like it?"

"Yeah." He frowned. "It's awfully wrinkled, though."

Grace looked down. She pulled it off, threw it on the bed, and walked out of the room. He was right—she should have taken it off before curling up in the window seat—but still it annoyed her that he'd pointed it out. That was why she hadn't told Diana. Not because Allison told her not to, but because Grace hadn't wanted Diana to point out all the wrinkles in the plan. Grace would have been forced to look too closely. She would have had to agree with Diana because she would have been right. Grace would have had to toss off the whole idea. And she hadn't wanted to. She'd wanted to try on something new. At least for a while.

Grace ducked under the rope and decided once and for all to talk to Stubblefield on Monday about the Japanese class. She needed an entirely new language.

Twice as many people were downstairs now. Diana was centered in a clump of them off in a corner. She lifted her arms over her head and wiggled her butt, and James Albee watched her. Grace knew she was telling the story about the belly dancer, and even though she couldn't actually hear it, Grace smiled at the punch line. She'd heard it many times before. She knew it by heart. It was a good story.

Allison's throaty laugh rose out of the sunroom. All Grace could see of her was a long white arm stretched out, poised like a red-tipped arrow. Giggles bubbled up around her. "Oh no!" one of her group yelled. "You're kidding!" Grace had no idea what Allison was telling them, and she couldn't help but wonder.

She splayed her fingers and studied her hands. The *Zo* was gone. She looked up and saw Ted, watching her from the kitchen, reflected in the mirror on the opposite wall.

Grace spun into the crowd, pulled into an orbit somewhere between the past and possibility.